DRIZZLE OF DEATH

CEECEE JAMES

For my Family— love you guys!

CONTENTS

Author's Note   vii

Blurb   ix

Chapter 1   1

Chapter 2   15

Chapter 3   29

Chapter 4   42

Chapter 5   49

Chapter 6   62

Chapter 7   69

Chapter 8   82

Chapter 9   92

Chapter 10   101

Chapter 11   107

Chapter 12   113

Chapter 13   120

Chapter 14   126

Chapter 15   131

Chapter 16   137

Chapter 17   144

Chapter 18   152

Chapter 19   159

Chapter 20   167

Chapter 21   175

Chapter 22   182

Chapter 23   189

Chapter 24   198

AUTHOR'S NOTE

This book is a work of fiction and although it does discuss events and places from the American Revolutionary War, the setting of the book is a fictional town utilizing facts from the war in order to enhance the story.

BLURB

Drizzle of Death by CeeCee James

What better thing to do on a beautiful spring morning than to explore the old world charm of an Amish village? Georgie Tanner takes her group of tourists on an exclusive visit to the local Amish township. With its stores and working water wheel, the group is impressed and fascinated by the amazing skills and peaceful lifestyle.

Georgie feels like she stepped back into a happier and safer time until she's pulled aside by one scared Amish girl. But Georgie never expected what the girl would tell her.

A young man, just returning from his Rumspringa, where he lived in the city, has been murdered. But Georgie must tread carefully with the information or the girl will be shunned by her community.

And then, just like that, everything is covered up, and the young witness is missing. But Georgie knows what she saw even though no one believes her. Now it's up to Georgie to find the missing girl. Who can she convince to help?

CHAPTER 1

It's amazing how much life can change in just a year-and-a-half. By *much* I mean, it's like looking back at a whole different person. A younger one and in more ways than just age.

That woman back then had long dirty-blonde hair that was highlighted every three months, a fiancé gorgeous enough to make her friends jealous, and a stuffed closet full of the newest trends. She kept her nails manicured and had a career as a paralegal at an estate attorney office.

And maybe had her nose in the air a bit.

I cringed at the memory. Some of the changes in my life had been horrible. My fiancé's death. I still could barely speak of it without feeling like I was talking about a nightmare.

But some changes had been very, very good. Sometimes, you don't know that you needed to grow until after it happens.

Anyway, here I am now, with my hair chopped to just below my jawline, squinting to read the directions on the instruction pamphlet from a box of hair dye. Brilliant Auburn, the box declared, with lowlights in one easy step.

One easy step. How hard can it be? I'd always gone to a hairdresser before, but my flat wallet was adamant that that option was out of the budget for a long time. I shook the pamphlet open to read it and then frowned at the tiny print. Were these warnings? A person would have to be the height of a Tic-Tac box for the words to appear normal size. After flipping the paper over, I discovered a film. What was this? Carefully, I peeled it away to reveal two floppy gloves and a hair cap.

I stared at myself in the mirror. The reflection looking back was not impressed. In fact (dare I say it?) there was a worry line, the same as the one my grandma always had, deep between my eyebrows.

Never mind. I can do this. I squared my shoulders and nodded at myself. Usually, when I worried about something, it was for nothing.

Now, this was a big change for me. I'd always been a blonde, so this new hair color was going to be a statement recognizing how I was a new person. The whole, I am woman, hear me roar, kind of thing.

It'd seemed like such a great idea last night while out to dinner with my best friend, Kari. Now I wondered if it hadn't been inspired by that second glass of red wine.

Just do it. It's only hair. It will grow back. Sighing, I grabbed the bottle and started shaking it.

My phone vibrated on the counter, making me jump. I'd forgotten I'd put it on silent mode after a telemarketer tried to convince me to apply for a new credit card that morning. I'd be embarrassed to admit the relief I felt at its interruption as I lunged to answer it.

"Hello?"

"GiGi?" Cecelia's sweet voice chimed out her nickname for me. I called the sixty-plus-year-old woman my aunt but we were actually no relation. She'd been my grandma's best friend before Grandma died and now employed me at her bed and breakfast as her tour guide. Like I said, big changes had happened to me.

"Hi, Cecelia." I set down the bottle, noting the way my fingers pushed it away. "How are you?"

"I'm good. Listen, I know this is kind of impromptu, but I

have guests here who were wondering if you could take them down to Sunny Acres. Do you have time?"

Do I have time? Hello, paycheck! "Of course! I'll be right over."

I'd just finished running a tour of Peach Creek—a war monument close to our town that was dedicated to the American Revolutionary heroes. Technically, I was off for the rest of the afternoon. But the winter months had really limited the tourists, which in turn had given my bank account a wallop, so I was eager for the work.

Besides, how could I tell Cecelia no? She'd been my rock ever since Derek had died.

Not to mention, I loved Sunny Acres, an Amish stopping place that had a bulk food store, a restaurant and some other buildings. It was about ten minutes outside of Gainesville, the town I lived in. Some of my favorite childhood memories were from Sunny Acres. Grandma loved to shop there for the heirloom tomatoes and other uncommon vegetables not found in the grocery store. While we were there, we'd always eat at the attached restaurant. I'd get the apple crisp. Grandma would sniff and mutter under her breath at me that her version was just as good and didn't cost seven dollars a pop. Then she'd take a bite of the homemade French vanilla bean ice-cream and grudgingly admit that maybe the price was worth it.

Grandma. I smiled every time I thought of her. Sweet but feisty, and always ready with a hug or a cookie. I had a pretty idyllic childhood despite the fact that my parents had died in a car accident when I was four. I had no memories of dad and very few of my mom. The clearest memory I had was the way the sun shone off her blonde hair one Easter morning. I cherished it, even though it made me sad that I didn't have more. And, to be honest, maybe a little guilty as well, like if I were a good daughter I'd remember everything.

But back to growing up—I didn't feel a lack in my childhood. Grandma loved me as much as any mother could. I had lots of freedom, with none of the distractions of cell phones or electronics. I played in the river, rode my bike, roller-skated and mercilessly teased Cecelia's grandson, Frank.

My smile got a little bigger at the thought of Frank. He'd grown from a knobby-kneed beanpole to a barrel-chested six-foot-plus man. And his sour attitude that had made him an easy target back in childhood had mellowed.

I pursed my lips, considering that statement. Well, somewhat mellowed, maybe. He was still a bit stodgy.

I swept my hair up into a stubby ponytail with a rubber band and then slipped on my shoes. The Baker Street Bed and Breakfast had only two couples staying this week. Both couples were retired and experienced travelers. It had been a relaxing time this morning at Peach Creek.

They were going to love Sunny Acres, I decided as I locked my apartment door. I jogged down the four flights to the ground floor, my legs finally used to the trek. It was a beautiful building but built well before the age of elevators. The historical preservation of the structure was one of my favorite things, and I still smiled as I ran my hand down the silky, polished wood banister.

I stepped on to the landing and whipped through the front door with its black security gate. The sun hit my face as I jogged to reach my van. Parking was scarce in downtown Gainesville, so I'd parked a couple of blocks away. Hurrying along, I passed Violet's Boutique, a cute clothing store that had mannequins on the curb that nearly blinded passersby with the sparkles on the jean's pockets. Violet was just returning from lunch and waved as I passed by.

Up ahead was my white van, which I referred to as "Old Bella." Usually, the name was said with a hint of fondness, but recently she'd left me stranded with not one, but two flat tires. So definitely more of an emphasis on *Old*.

I unlocked and climbed into the van, immediately bombarded by the scent of barbecue sauce. The van had once been used as a catering vehicle, and the barbecue part of that business had left a lasting legacy.

The drive to Cecelia's business was lovely as usual. She lived right at the edge of town, on a street surrounded by gorgeous maple trees. Spring and summer saw them dressed in leafy green splendor, changing to a patchwork red in the fall. A thrill of happiness shot through me now as I spotted tiny leaf buds on the branches.

I parked the van in her driveway and ran up the porch stairs, pushing the porch swing to make it sway as I passed, and then opened the front door.

The living room was dark. Flickering candlelight reflected off the wall.

"Cecelia?" I called out, surprised.

"GiGi!" She came bustling around the corner, her white hair pulled high in its characteristic bun and her dress covered with a checkered apron. "Did you see anything on the way here?"

"Anything? What do you mean?"

"Yes, like the power company."

I frowned, thinking. "No, I actually didn't. When did the power go out?"

"About a second after I hung up with you. What's worse is that I'm in the middle of baking a cheesecake."

"Luckily, not before I got my coffee," said Mr. Stevens, one of the guests staying there. He took a sip from his mug and the candlelight showed his appreciative grin.

"Like you need the caffeine at this time of day," his wife chided, coming from behind him. The married couple was unusual in that they both dressed in the same clothes, a blue hoody, t-shirt, and khakis. The only difference was the color of their shoes and their height, which was dramatic. He'd proudly claimed to be six foot seven, while his wife looked up from the region of his armpit.

Mr. Stevens hurriedly gulped the remaining coffee. His wife's lips pursed together in disapproval at the sound.

"I guess the Walters wanted to stay back," Cecelia said, referring to the other guests.

"Great! Well, I'm ready to leave when you are," I nodded to the Stevens while jiggling my keys. I stopped in mid jiggle, realizing it sounded like I was trying to rush them.

"You all set?" Mrs. Stevens asked her husband. He started for the kitchen with his mug.

"I can take that for you," Cecelia said with a smile. "Have dishes piling up that need to be taken care of. Give me something to do while I'm waiting for the power to come back on."

The couple followed me out to Old Bella with me muttering

a silent prayer that she would start. This time, she didn't give me any trouble, and once the Stevens had strapped their seat belts on, we were on our way.

Sunny Acres Market brimmed with color despite the more monochromatic clothing of the people who ran the bustling event. Sturdy wooden booths with cedar awning covered tables were crammed full of vegetables, baked goods, and flowers. Scattered among them were the hand-made items the Amish community produced in their everyday lives.

The three of us entered the market. Mr. Stevens nibbled something from a sampling tray while his wife sniffed the brightly colored petals of the cut flowers. Mr. Stevens carried his sample over to one of the rocking chairs and sat down. I couldn't help smiling. I'd always been fascinated with the rocking chairs. They were gorgeous with the sheen of the wood grain glowing in the light. Some day, I was going to own one.

"Those are amazing, aren't they?" I said.

He rocked with a nostalgic smile on his face. "Reminds me of Sunday dinners after church."

Mrs. Stevens plopped into the chair next to his and pointed to the building at the far end of the market. "What's that over there?"

I glanced over using my hand to shield my eyes from the sun.

"That's the old mill." With that, I broke into my practiced narration about the history of the mill, its uses and functions, and then the tragic accident that had occurred in the late 1800s, when a young pre-teen fell out of the top loft hatchway onto the wheel, losing consciousness before he even hit the icy waters below.

"Oh my," Mrs. Stevens gasped. She held a hand up to her mouth as she stared at the still operating water wheel. "They worked them so young back then. What a shame."

Mr. Stevens joined her with a solemn nod.

I continued, "It was later discovered that the boy had been pushed. A witness came forward saying he'd seen the boy arguing with a young man. After poking around, the man became a suspect when it was learned that he had been robbing the mill by stealing portions of each load that went out. The boy was going to tell the mill boss when he was instructed that someone needed him in the loft. There, the thief pushed the boy out the hatch. The case was sealed when they found the stolen wood at the thief's home, hidden in an old barn, and a handkerchief with his initials sewn into the corner found in the loft near the open doorway."

"What if it was just coincidence or accident?" Mrs. Stevens asked.

"A coincidence, Judith?" Mr. Stevens snorted.

"Not in their eyes. You see, in the Amish community, the Amish believe it is up to the sinner to come forward and repent for their crimes. They believe that almost any crime committed can be redeemed as long as the sinner is honest with himself, the church, and God. And so, weeks later, the young man confessed. He was shunned from attending meetings for several weeks, as his crime resulted in another human being unable to seek solace in the church. Once his shunning was complete, the young man was allowed to carry on his life within the community, although he was expected to contribute more to make up for the life he had taken."

"He wasn't punished?" Mrs. Steven's eyebrows rose in horror. She shook her head. "At least the times have changed. They would never get away with murder now."

"That's not exactly true," Mr. Stevens spoke up again. "Even today, the Amish don't involve outside government and laws. They handle everything themselves, including dealing out any punishment. I watched a documentary where they said it's highly frowned upon, even forbidden, for the Amish people to go outside of their own community for any help, including for criminal acts."

"Even murder? In this day and age?" Mrs. Stevens crossed her arms.

"Murder is super rare," I broke in. "They consider it the worst crime that can be committed. In fact, only one person from an

Amish community has ever been arrested, tried and convicted for murder."

This didn't seem to reassure Mrs. Stevens.

I pressed forward with more optimism. "Living a life serving in their religious beliefs is important to the Amish. They have a simple life compared to ours, but that doesn't mean issues don't arise. Usually, it's money issues, drugs, and so on. But they do strive to live peacefully and honestly."

She still wasn't smiling so I decided to change the subject. We walked around the market area for a bit, ending close to the water wheel.

I continued my lesson, more out of muscle memory than anything else. "Though this mill is still operational in a functioning sense, it hasn't been used as a sawmill in decades. The Amish keep everything running and maintained for the tourists."

They stared at the water splashing from bucket to bucket. I was happy to see them appreciating it.

I loved the water mill. When I was little, I'd thrown pennies into it. And when I ran out of pennies, rocks. Grandma had been none too pleased when she'd caught me, and her lips had tightened into the "we're in public, but you wait until I get you into the car" smile. That scolding was my first lesson about respecting other peoples' belongings.

Mrs. Stevens looked a little bleak from the discussion, but I hoped to get her back on track by exploring more of Sunny Acres Market, with its shelves stocked with flour, bread, and other bulk raw ingredients and baked goods. As we wandered, I eyed a cheesecake. I wasn't sure if the power cutting out in mid-baking cycle would ruin the one Cecelia was making, but I figured having an extra cheesecake couldn't hurt. And she always had a fondness for the baked goods from "the old mill."

I grabbed the pan and headed over to the counter where two Amish girls sat, one knitting and the other mending a pair of pants with a wicker basket piled with clothing by her feet. Both of the girls wore black bonnets and looked to be in their very early teens. The sewer's eyes were red as though she'd been crying. As I approached, the knitter nudged the sewer.

"Hello," I said, trying to hide my curiosity. I set the cheesecake on the table and searched in my purse for my wallet. I was a little embarrassed when I pulled it out, with its broken snap closure flapping open.

"Eight dollars, please," said the knitter.

The second girl's eyes locked on to mine for a moment, and her lips trembled. Then her gaze cut back to the pants in her hands.

Something about that look grabbed my heart. "Are you okay?" I asked her gently.

The knitter frowned at her friend as she took my cash. Quickly, she counted out the change and handed it back to me. I deposited the bills into the mill donation box, hesitating to leave until the girl answered me.

The young girl slowly stood up. Her gaze caught mine again, and she waved me to follow.

"Mary...." The knitter's eyes tightened as she stared at her friend.

The young girl ignored her friend and headed toward the back of the store.

"Mary, I'm not covering for you," the knitter warned.

The girl glanced back to see if I was following her. She waved again, just two fingers that slightly moved. But the expression on her face showed it was urgent.

At this point, I hadn't even agreed to follow. But something in her eyes set my feet in motion. I picked up the cheesecake pan and went after her.

The black-bonneted teen led me all the way through the store, not looking back again.

Where was she taking me?

CHAPTER 2

*T*he stairway she led me to was at the furthest point from the store's open doors. I was curious, but also felt a few prickles of apprehension dance along my neck as I followed her. It wasn't often that the Amish would have private discussions with people outside of their community. I'd certainly never had any before.

The young girl moved around a stack of empty wood boxes and into an alcove behind the stairway. She beckoned me inside the nook and then turned, her hands brushing down her dark skirt as she studied the path we had just come from. Satisfied, she glanced at me, making brief eye contact before dropping her gaze to the floor.

"My name is Georgie," I began. "How can I help you?"

"I heard you talking earlier." Her voice was soft and I had to lean in closer to listen. "I've seen you here before. You seem to have an understanding of our ways. You do history tours, right?"

"Yes." I nodded, wondering where the girl was going.

"Sometimes," she hesitated, and her tongue dotted her top lip. Then she straightened her spine and continued. "Sometimes things occur that should probably involve others who are not of our community. But at the same time, we should never seek outsiders out."

I nodded again, even more confused than before.

She glanced back into the store, and I was disturbed to see her face pale. I could see her swallowing hard, and when she looked back at me, her eyes were huge and dark. "But maybe it's possible to ask an outsider for help, secretively? And that person might be able to give an oath to listen and not tell anyone?"

Alarm shot through me. "Did someone hurt you?"

"No, no. No one hurt me." She gave a tight smile, her gaze still darting back into the store, keeping track of anyone who might be approaching. She reached toward my sleeve as if to pull me in deeper behind the stairwell but stopped short just before touching me. "You must realize that even by talking with you, I risk being shunned. But I'm desperate." Her eyes magnified as they filled with tears. How old was this girl? Seeing her hands twisting the corner of her apron, she now looked to be only ten or twelve.

Her bottom lip quivered and I promptly decided. "I'll help you however I can."

"You will keep it a secret?"

I knew she wouldn't say more unless I agreed. I nodded, hoping it was a promise I could really keep.

Relief caused her cheeks to flush. "It's my friend, Jacob. He had a fight with some outsiders in a field a few days ago. They said that it was just a misunderstanding and he spooked at nothing but..." She sighed and her hand fluttered to her chest.

"Who's *they*? And what do you think happened?"

She peeked around the corner again, the cords standing out in her neck in anxiety. Seeing nothing, she leaned back to whisper, "The Elders. Jacob's been known to have issues. He got himself into trouble during his Rumspringa. He met an English woman during that time."

I knew the term, Rumspringa. It was the season the Amish had their young adults experience the real world before choosing the Amish lifestyle permanently.

Mary tucked a wisp of hair back into her bonnet. "My uncle found him in town and had a few stern words with him. It was then that Jacob decided to end his Rumspringa and the English to return to our town. I thought he would be doing better." Her bottom lip trembled. "But he's had an accident. He's fallen."

"Fallen?" I glanced to see if he were nearby. "Where is he, now?"

"Mary!" A male voice called over my shoulder, making me jump. "Why are you neglecting your duties?"

Mary paled and seemed to shrink to half her size as her shoulders bowled in. I peered around the boxes to see a man towering over the top of me by over a foot. Now I am only five-foot-two, so that's not saying much. But the man's girth was nearly two of me as well, covered with a black broadcloth held shut with a leather belt. His busy eyebrows shadowed tiny, beetle-like eyes that shifted away from me as if I were inconsequential.

Mary darted around me and back into the store, her boots scarcely making a sound on the wooden boards.

The man exhaled loudly and his nose flared. Positioning his hat more firmly on his head, he turned and followed her without another look in my direction.

What was that about?

I stood there, clutching my cheesecake, wondering what in

the world just happened. Shaking my head, I followed them as well.

Back in the noise and bustle of the main store, I spotted the blue sweatshirts of the Stevens'. They were still puttering around, with Mrs. Stevens holding a quilt and talking animatedly with her husband. Mr. Stevens rolled his eyes but his hand rubbed the base of her back, showing a deep love.

I looked for Mary at the checkout and was disappointed to see she hadn't returned there. Where had the girl run off to? I surveyed the store for the intimidating man, but he seemed to have disappeared as well.

Very strange.

I walked to the front door, feeling kind of lost. Quickly, I brought the cheesecake out to the van and then headed back inside to search for the girl. There were black bonnets, and a few white ones, scattered among the aisles but none proved to be Mary.

I meandered to the rear of the store, where a breeze came through the opened back door and ruffled some aprons that were displayed on a wooden rack. I walked to the doorway and stared at the field freshly plowed under.

The air was clean and cool, and I stepped outside into the sunshine. Suddenly, my skin tingled like I was being watched. I almost felt like I was about to get into trouble, and didn't dare glance back, afraid to see someone about to sound the alarm.

I'm not doing anything wrong, just getting a breath of fresh air.

Squinting in the bright light, I walked along the side of the building so no one could see me. From behind me were the happy voices of the customers, but it was quiet out here, other than the call of birds.

Footsteps from my left caught my attention. It was Mary, racing for the wheelhouse. She disappeared into the old building.

I watched the door shut behind her and then went after her. After that weird conversation, I needed some answers.

The sun beat against my back as I hurried along the path. A grasshopper sprang out in front of me, startling me. He was out early this year.

The wheelhouse was dark with age and heavy with the smell of mulchy earth. Cautiously, I approached and pushed the door open, wincing as it let out a creak.

Two small windows allowed sunbeams to dimly light the room. The glass panes were not nearly as old as the building and must have been recently updated. Along the back wall was a fireplace made of smooth rock. Black soot streaked the top of the mantle.

I blinked a few times, trying to force my eyes to adjust to the muted light. Mary was nowhere in sight. A board squealed under my foot, and I froze. There was no way I was going in further.

Swallowing hard, I called out. My voice cracked. "Hello? Everything okay in here?"

"Oh, thank the Lord!" Mary shouted. "Please, come down here!"

I turned toward her voice and spotted a set of stairs. She was somewhere down there. "Mary? What's going on?"

"It's Jacob." The girl's voice was high with worry.

Gripping the handrail, I walked down the stairs, my mouth dropping open as I passed a boot on one of the treads. It was a man's boot, sitting on its side with laces untied. Drops of dark liquid marred the wood surface.

My muscles tensed. At the bottom was a young man with his face partially covered by one arm. Mary knelt by his side.

"What happened?" I clattered down the rest of the way.

"This is what I was trying to get help for. No one will help him because he's drunk."

The boy's breathing was slow and shallow. Alarm zipped along my spine. "He needs a doctor immediately."

"I tried. Elder Yoder said to leave him. That Jacob needed to learn a lesson." She patted the young man's face. "Jacob! Can you hear me?"

The boy didn't respond. An enormous lump stood out on his forehead.

"He could have a concussion," I said. "He might have a brain injury."

"Jacob!" the girl sobbed.

"Can we go around Elder Yoder's rule? Maybe get a friend of his? Anyone else?"

She looked at me, her large eyes fringed with wet lashes. "To go against the elder risks getting shunned. No one will do it."

I watched the young man struggle to breathe and reached for my cell phone. "I can get help."

She saw my phone and jumped to grab my arm. "No! Don't! You risk my whole family!"

I hesitated. "What about his mom? Can you get her?

The girl nodded. "I'll find her right now. Promise you won't call?"

I gritted my teeth and nodded. She flew up the stairs. As the door banged open, I let out a sigh.

Looking down at the young man, a wave of sorrow washed over me. The poor kid. He looked to be a late teen or in his very early twenties. His hair was cut in a different style than the other Amish men I'd seen at Sunny Acres. I studied his outstretched arm and paused. There was a tan line on his wrist. One that would have been made by a watch band.

I examined him a little more, noting the knot on his head, and then glanced at the stairs. It wasn't an open wound. So where had the blood come from? And how had his boot come off? I sniffed hard, noting the lack of the scent of alcohol.

Something wasn't right.

Gently, I tipped his head so that his chin pointed up, trying to ease his breathing. I juggled my cell phone, unsure of what to do. Should I really wait to call for help? I decided to give her a few minutes and then I would call, no matter what she said. In the meanwhile, I snapped a few pictures in case the police would need them. First of how his body lay on the floor, then of his bare foot, then the few drops of blood on the stairs, and finally of the boot.

The door swung open, making me jump. A man was there, the same man who had cornered Mary and me at the stairs.

"English!" he yelled, before turning to spurt off something I couldn't understand. One hand was in his pocket, but the other had hold of Mary's arm. He pulled her into view. Her face was frozen in terror, and she quickly waved a hand at me.

"Please come up," she said. "We will take care of it from here."

I froze at the hostility in the man's eyes. He shouted a command I couldn't understand but it prompted me to scurry up the stairs. He barely took a step back to allow me to pass him. His hair dripped from sweat, and the salty scent rolled off of him. He glared at me, his lip curled in disgust, before yelling at Mary again. She squeezed small and passed me to hurry down the stairs to Jacob.

"You go, now," the man commanded.

"What about the boy? He needs a doctor," I asked.

"We take care of our own." With every word, he used his bulk to edge me toward the door. I back-pedaled over the threshold.

"Mary said no one was helping. That someone wanted him to learn his lesson," I said. "He may have a brain injury."

"We take care of our own," he growled again. With one more parting stare at me, he slammed the door.

I stood on the stoop, feeling bewildered. What do I do, now? Just act as though everything was fine? Call the police?

I decided to text Frank. He was a deputy with the Gainesville police. The gravel crunched under my shoes as I walked back to the Sunny Acres store. The young knitter glanced up from her project as I walked by.

The Stevens were walking toward the check-out stand as I approached. The quilt draped over Mrs. Steven's arm, and she smiled like she'd just won a huge battle.

"You guys ready?" I asked, feeling anxious. I wiped sweaty hands on my pants and glanced around for the ogre of a man.

They nodded and went to pay for the quilt. I pulled out my phone to text Frank.

Frank's and my relationship had changed a lot through the years, from when we use to tease each other mercilessly, to our last summer in high school where we volunteered to work with the city's homeless. At the end of that summer, we'd both moved away—me to the city where I became engaged to Derek, and Frank to the army. Eventually, Frank returned home after receiving a medical discharge for an injury that occurred in Afghanistan. His vehicle had run over the top of an IED, and to this day, he carried shrapnel in his chest.

I returned the year after he did, numb and broken myself from Derek's death, having literally watched my fiancé's car fly down an embankment. I can't describe the horror of standing at the top of the road, screaming his name. Trying to call his cell phone, call the police, chained in helplessness while his car billowed black smoke.

The fire marshal had ruled it a suicide, which I never believed. Derek had been more content than I'd ever seen him. The only thing that had been on his mind was his new job.

But nothing I said could sway the verdict. And so, after the funeral, I came back to the only home I knew. Cecelia had taken me in, and Frank along with her.

The thought of Frank made me shake my head. As much as he was a curmudgeon, he also had an awful sweet side. He sure tried to keep it hidden but—bit by bit—I'd dug it out. I have to admit, he was more comforting than I ever dared to admit. He really was a rock to lean on, despite his grouchy side.

And I was needing some support right about now.

I quickly texted. —**Frank. I have a hurt kid and no one wants to help.**

He wrote back.—**You try 911?**

Like I said. Full of compassion. I rolled my eyes before typing, —**It's complicated. They don't want help. Can you come to Sunny Acres?**

His response,—**He's a kid?**

Come on. Come on. Quit giving me a hard time and just drive. I bit my lip and furiously typed. — **Don't know for sure given that he's unconscious. But I pretty much got kicked off the property. Now get over here.**

I thought about it for a second and added, —**please.**

He sent back a grumpy face. An actual grumpy face. While I was trying to interpret what that meant, a second text came in. —**On my way.**

"We're ready!" Mrs. Stevens said, showing up nearly at my elbow. I jumped since I hadn't noticed her approaching. "Oh, sorry! I didn't mean to scare you," she apologized.

I smiled and lifted my phone. "I was totally focused in this text. Bad habit, I guess."

She answered airily, "Well, that's not something I've ever been that interested in. We usually just call when we need someone."

I nodded. "You ready to get in the van?"

Both she and her husband walked across the parking lot to Old Bella. I threw up another Hail Mary, hoping the van would start and followed after them.

I was about half-way into the driver's seat when I saw Mary again.

"Hang on just a sec," I said to the Stevens. "I'll be right back."

By the time I climbed back out, the girl was disappearing around the building. My stomach sank. I was going to lose her again.

CHAPTER 3

*L*eaving the door to the van open, I sprinted across the parking lot, desperate to catch up with the Amish girl.

"Mary!" I called. My voice sounded unnaturally loud and I cringed at the attention it gathered.

She turned at the sound of her name. Her eyes were red from crying. She wiped the back of her hand under her nose and waited for me to reach her.

I ran up, suddenly was at a loss for words. What was I going to say?

"How's Jacob?" I settled on, lamely.

"He's...he's going to be fine." Her eyes were glassy as she gave the pronouncement.

I was stunned. "Fine? Are you sure?"

She sniffed and nodded her head. "He was talking when I left."

Words spun around in my head like the letters in a boiling pot of alphabet soup. "Are you sure?"

She nodded, her bottom lip trembling. "Yes. The doctor and Elder Yoder are with him. Elder Yoder will make sure everything is okay. He wants nothing to sully the Amish name."

Sully the Amish name? "Okay..." I nodded, feeling confused. "Uh, If there's anything I can do..." I stopped, helpless. What could I do to help her? Give her my phone number? She couldn't use it to get hold of me. My offer to help was just a useless gesture.

She seemed to understand my heart though and gave me a small smile. "Jacob will be okay. We all will be. But it's important to remember that life comes and life goes like the weeds thrown into the fire."

My eyes narrowed. She'd recited the parable as if she'd just heard it.

"Weeds? What do you mean?"

"Elder Yoder just told me it. He is taking care of poor Jacob."

"How is he taking care of Jacob?" I asked. "I thought you said it was a doctor?"

"I have to go." Her gaze darted to the left. "I can't talk with you anymore. I've been told to get back to my task. Disobeying an elder risks getting shunned."

"Okay." I backed away feeling numb. That was the third time she'd brought up the word "shunned." I watched Mary travel across the yard and walk into the store, the heels of her boots clacking against the wooden floor as she entered.

Feeling slightly defeated, I walked back to the van. Mary's puffy eyes contradicted her statement that Jacob was okay. She was lying to me. But why?

I climbed into the van and held my keys. When a good idea didn't spring to mind, I bit my lip and started the van. There was nothing more that I could do. Hopefully, Frank would soon be here to sort it out.

I texted him one more time. —**Have to bring the guests back to the B&B. Look for a girl named Mary. She can take you to Jacob.**

Sighing, I hit send.

"You guys ready to go home?" I asked, smiling into the rearview mirror.

Mr. Stevens nodded, one eyebrow raised. "Five hundred dollars," he said, holding up a corner of the quilt. Mrs. Stevens rolled her eyes. "After a splurge like this, I'm not sure we can afford to be on vacation any longer."

As I RATTLED down the Baker Street Bed and Breakfast's driveway, I could tell from the dark windows that the power was still off.

Mrs. Stevens spouted out, "Well, time to live like the Amish for a day, I guess!" The couple climbed out, chattering away about the card game they were planning for later.

I checked my phone and rolled my eyes. Still no text from Frank.

Oscar, Cecelia's widowed next door neighbor, was standing on his porch. I glanced around for Peanut, the Pomeranian that Oscar insisted on calling Bear. The old man hated the name, Peanut, but it had been given to the dog by his wife and was the only name the animal answered to. I often heard him holler, "Bear!" before begrudgingly muttering "Peanut," in a much quieter voice.

Today was no different. Peanut was staring up a tree, barking hysterically at a squirrel. The dog badly needed a trip to the groomers and looked like a giant cotton ball hopping on stubby legs.

"Bear! Get over here! Leave that fluffy-tailed rat alone! Bear!" Oscar let out a few dark words before hissing out, "Confound it. Peanut! Come here you little treat-eating monster." His last words came out at a much higher pitch as if he were pleased with the dog. But the look in his eyes showed he was about at the end of his patience.

The dog ignored his plea. Oscar started down the stairs when I stopped him. I knew how bad his arthritis was.

"I'll get her," I assured him and jogged over to the tree.

The dog's dark eyes sparkled with excitement when she saw me. She pranced back and forth, happy to share her arch-enemy with me.

"Yes. I see him," I said, squatting down. "He's a big, bad squirrel, isn't he? Come here, Peanut."

The dog ran over, after giving the squirrel one last defiant bark. The squirrel fluffed its tail and ran along a branch, chittering away.

I scooped up the pup and carried her to the house. A few leaves clung to her fur.

"No wonder she doesn't come when I call her, with you coddling her like a rag doll," Oscar said, his brow creasing into a frown. I handed the dog over and he took her with a huff. He turned his back to me to bring her inside, but not before I saw him pick out a leaf with red, arthritic fingers. Softly, he stroked the dog around the ears before setting her inside with a "Scoot!"

"So, how are you doing, today, Oscar?" I asked, leaning against the porch railing. I had to admire the paint. Frank and I had spent a couple of weeks pressure washing and scraping the old paint off, and now it gleamed in a fresh white coat.

"Doing? I'm alive and breathing, so that's something. But I guess I'd be a whole lot better if I had an apple turnover." His eyes widened innocently at me but I wasn't fooled. He'd caught the scent of cinnamon apples coming from Cecelia's kitchen this morning.

I laughed. "I'll see what I can do. And maybe I can bring Bear to the groomers later."

"Groomers!" He stepped back, alarmed. "What in tarnation would you do that for? Dog's already got a big head. She doesn't need to get all frou-frou on top of it."

I tried my best to hide my smile. "Just to get the hair-mats and stickers out. She seems to have a few."

"Went off her rocker and chased after the squirrel into those darn blackberries. That dog is more bush than animal, now."

"Well, let me take care of it. Then she won't be tracking stuff into your house."

He raised an eyebrow at me as if to remind me of the appearance of his bachelor pad. But the dinging of my phone saved me, and I pulled it out to see a text from Frank. I waved goodbye and headed back to Cecelia's, with Oscar hollering after me to keep my eye out for any stray turnovers.

Frank's text read.—**I'm here at Sunny Acres. No one knows what you're talking about. Where are you?**

What in the world? Alarm prickled through me. —**Had to leave. Did you talk with Mary?**

Frank responded, —**It's an Amish community. Any guesses on many Marys there are? Just get down here already.**

I frowned. He seemed grumpier than usual. —**On my way.**

I'd have to get Oscar his turnovers later. I climbed into the van and drove back to Sunny Acres.

———

THE PARKING LOT was even fuller than earlier this afternoon. Exiting my van, I saw a police car parked near the entrance of the establishment. A horse harnessed to its buggy swished his tail and stepped skittishly as I passed by.

Where was Frank? I started toward the grocery building when I saw a figure dressed in blue waving frantically at me from a group of trees about twenty yards away.

"Mary!" I smiled as I approached. She glanced at me shyly, then dipped her head, before hiding behind one of the trees. I followed after her, concern growing.

"Hi," I said. "How are you doing?"

She drew me into the group of trees. Standing next to her was another young woman also dressed in blue. I hesitated to ask about Jacob in front of the new person, not sure if I'd be getting her into trouble.

"Thank you for coming over here. This is my friend, Naomi." Naomi had the similar blue eyes and dark hair as her friend.

"Hello. I'm Georgie."

Naomi nodded, her eyes dipping as often as her friend's.

Mary continued in a whisper, "The police are here. I'm scared." Freckles stood out on her pale cheeks.

"I get it. I understand." I reached to pat her shoulder but she pulled away before I could touch her. Darn it. When would I remember not everyone likes to be touched? "I bet it feels scary having the police here. Don't worry. They just want to make sure everyone is safe, and figure out what happened to Jacob."

Mary flinched at the boy's name.

I pressed forward, "Is he okay?"

She twisted the corner of her apron and licked her bottom lip. Naomi stared at her friend as if waiting for the answer as well. Finally, the young girl whispered, "He is with elder Yoder. They are bringing in a doctor."

"You told me a doctor was already with him." I took a step back.

Her eyes widened with fright at my sudden movement. "Elder Yoder told me so. I haven't really seen him, since..."

"Since I was there?"

She nodded. "Elder Yoder said the drink must wear off and Jacob would be fine." She looked uncertain.

"But you don't think so?"

At this point Naomi interrupted. "He swore he wouldn't drink again, not after what happened."

"What happened?" I asked.

Both girls looked at each other, their eyes wide.

"We don't want to make improper assumptions or think ill of anyone. It isn't our place to judge." Mary responded. Naomi nodded, her face pale.

"I understand. But something has you concerned. I know I'm English, and I can understand why you're having a hard time letting me in. But if you want my help, I need to know more. Why did you come find me? Do you think someone had a reason to hurt Jacob? I remember you said he'd just returned from... what was it called? Rum—"

"From Rumspringa. He came back a few days ago."

"Did he make any friends while he was out there?"

"Jacob said he kissed a girl." Mary's cheeks flushed. "He wanted to see what it was like. He did not know the girl was with someone. She had a boyfriend, he said. He was confused and hurt by it, which is why he told me."

"I see." I paused, trying not to question the girls too harshly. They acted like a pair of skittish colts. "Do you think that boyfriend was angry with Jacob?"

"He came to our town, in his truck, and started yelling about someone 'messing with his girl' and 'taking something that belonged to him.' We think he had been drinking. He was kicking things and throwing things. Brother Jonathan and Brother David walked him to his truck and told him he would need to leave. He tried hitting one of them. Eventually, a few others came out and made him get in his truck and go away."

"So the boyfriend was mad, then." I glanced at the wheelhouse, hoping to see Frank so I could flag him over. There was no one.

The girls caught me looking. Mary grabbed my sleeve. Her hand fell away immediately when I turned toward her. "Please. You said you wouldn't tell anyone."

I nodded, with a slight smile. Obviously, she was going to have to talk to the police, but I didn't want her to be scared. I tried to build more of a rapport between us. "What did you think when the man showed up?"

Again the girls glanced at each other. Naomi answered, "I thought he was a buffoon."

"A... buffoon?" The word made me smile.

"Yes. He couldn't hardly stand. Drink made him like a child."

"So you weren't scared?"

The girls shook their head.

"But then there was the..." Mary started to say, tucking a wisp under her black head covering.

"Mary!" Naomi hissed.

I straightened my shoulders. Maybe tough love was needed after all. "Ladies, something happened here. Something serious. You owe it to your friend to figure out what happened. What if the person isn't done taking out his revenge?"

That seemed to convince Naomi. Her head bobbed quickly, giving Mary permission to continue.

"Two days ago, one of Jacob's family's buggy was set on fire. And other bad things were happening."

Naomi patted Mary's shoulder as the girl's eyes squeezed shut. Tears flowed down her face, but she didn't make a sound.

I pressed a little harder, "Was the boyfriend the only one? Is it possible Jacob made someone else angry when he was outside?" I didn't know if outside was the right word, but they seemed to understand what I meant.

Naomi bobbed her head. "There was another man. He's English and lives in the field with the large red silo. Jacob had been playing in one of the man's tractors and it began to roll. It's forbidden to operate such machinery, and Jacob wouldn't know how. He was being rebellious. He asked God for forgiveness so much afterward. The tractor went into the pond and Jacob had to swim out. The man was furious. He told Jacob's parents that Jacob would have to buy him a new one. We have no way to get anything like that. They made an agreement, but I don't know much about it."

"Is that where the gang of boys attacked him?" I looked at Mary.

She nodded.

I reached into my purse and texted Frank. —**You here?**

"There's someone I'd like you to talk with," I said as I pushed send.

Naomi jerked her head up while Mary stared in horror at my phone.

"You said we could talk with you," Mary whispered.

"I'll keep you safe. I promise." I said with a reassuring smile. "You both did so well. I just need you to share it with...."

At those words, the two girls took off. I watched them as they raced down the field, helpless to make them stop.

CHAPTER 4

The young girls disappeared into the tree line. I kept a close eye on them, hoping to at least have a direction in which I could point Frank. Then, with a sigh, I walked back toward the wheelhouse.

My phone buzzed as I approached the building's door.

—I saw your van. Frank was to the point as ever.

My text was a little longer. **—Standing outside the well door. Just lost two possible witnesses.**

He didn't text back. His response was a thundering of footsteps through the wheelhouse. A moment later, the door slammed open.

Frank raised an eyebrow as he caught sight of me. The man

was nearly inhuman. He didn't even squint in the bright sunlight.

"Where are they?" he asked.

"Hi, yourself," I said, cheerfully, to which he ignored. "They are two scared girls, and they ran that way." I took a step back so I could point toward the forest.

His eyes followed my finger while speaking into his shoulder mic.

"So, you found him," I said, crossing my arms.

His face was expressionless as he turned toward me. He stood nearly a foot taller than my measly five-foot-two, making me look up. I sidestepped so his head could be blocking the sun.

"Well?" I prompted. "Is an ambulance coming?"

"No one's coming. That's because we didn't see anybody." His nostrils flared. "I told you, no one's confessing to knowing what you're talking about."

My mouth dropped in shock. "You were serious with that message. I thought you were kidding." I stopped. Of course Frank wasn't kidding. The guy wasn't known for his sense of humor. As kids, we used to call him stick-in-the-mud, because of his permanent dourness.

"Nope. No hurt young man, boy, whatever. And that Elder

guy seems to think you're a trouble-maker. But, oddly the whole area smells like a chemical. Maybe lye? This whole thing stinks to high heaven."

"Did you show them the pictures?" I asked.

He wrinkled his nose as he looked at me. "What pictures?"

"What do you mean? Did I forget to send them?" I scrambled for my phone and quickly dialed them up.

Then I groaned.

The pictures were dark. I tried to blow them up but you couldn't make out much other than the shape of a person. Even the ones on the stairs were too dark to make out any identifying details.

Frank took my phone from my hand and stared.

"It's not like there was a light I could turn on," I said defensively. "Maybe I can play around with them to make them lighter."

He clenched his jaw. "Sure, you can play around with them. But, once you start messing with them, they won't be admissible in any court of law. Tampering with evidence."

"But you can see it, right?"

His eyes softened, and he reached for my shoulder. "Of course, Georgie. I don't doubt you at all. But you can imagine how our hands are tied. We can't go traipsing around here, not without probable cause. The Amish deal with things on their own, out here."

Some more footfalls pounded up the stairs. Soon Jefferson joined Frank and me. Elder Yoder was there too, his eyebrows appearing like wild briar bushes that had just attached themselves to his face. He glowered at me and licked his bottom lip. The same hand was still jammed into his pocket.

"This is my friend who talked with the girl," Frank indicated me with a jerk of his chin. "The girl's name is Mary, and she ran that way. You know who she is?"

"Mary?" Elder Yoder huffed. His eyes locked on my mine. "In a community this wide, there are many young girls christened Mary. Surely you have some more information. I'm sorry but I canna' guess who she's talking about."

My blood ran cold at his denial. "The one who was at these very steps." I pointed, my finger trembling with anger. "With you."

He looked over his shoulder at the staircase and then back at me. His mouth twisted into a sneer. "Well, ye can see for yourself there's no one there."

I bit my tongue, hating this nasty man. I didn't want to give him more information, afraid it would go badly for her.

I turned to Frank. "There was a girl inside the store who knows her. Maybe we can go see if she'll be more cooperative."

"Nay, you have no reason to be harassing my patrons and people," Elder Yoder said.

"Listen up." Frank took a step toward him. "Like it or not, we're here. And we do have photographic evidence. If you don't cooperate, it would only take a judge two seconds to issue a warrant and the whole squad of us would descend here. And we'd pick this place apart, let me tell you. Who knows how many secrets we'd find."

Elder Yoder lifted his chest. His expression hardened as his hands rose. One was bandaged but that didn't seem to stop him from clenching it into a powerful fist. "You English always butt in where ye don't belong." Then with a sarcastic smile. "As you wish." He gestured toward the store with a sweaty palm.

I led Frank and Jefferson to the cash register where I'd earlier bought my cheesecake. The knitter was still there. As soon as she saw us, the young woman got up to walk away.

"Ester," Elder Yoder called. "Ye have no reason to fear. I'm here. Just answer the questions for the English lady." His smile sent chills down my spine.

"Hi, there. Remember me?" I gave her my most disarming smile.

She shook her head, her eyes wide like an owl's.

I frowned. "I was just in here an hour ago. I bought some cheesecake?"

Again, the head shake.

"Ye can' not be bothering them if they have no recollect. We have hundreds of customers. To us, all you English look alike." His lip curled in disdain to show what he thought of us.

I tried harder. "There was a girl who was sitting with you. She asked me to come talk to her. Where is she now?"

The young woman paled and twined a bit of yarn around her finger. "I see many people. I can't say where she is."

My eyes narrowed at her word usage. She wasn't lying after all. She really couldn't say.

It quickly became obvious we weren't going to get any more information. I didn't bother to ask anyone else. As soon as the Amish workers saw Elder Yoder, they shied away.

Officer Jefferson made one more attempt at getting information. "Listen, Miss Tanner here says she saw a seriously injured young man. We'd really like to know where he is."

Elder Yoder's brow wrinkled as though puzzled. "If we had an injured young man, I'm sure he's at his home in our doctor's care. We don't expect the English to get involved in our affairs. Now, if I can excuse myself."

"Can you direct us to his home so that we can see for ourselves?"

"Truly, how would I know where he's gone off to? He's of accountable age."

Jefferson stiffened, and I could see he was struggling, but there was nothing any of us could do.

CHAPTER 5

The investigation ended rather abruptly, with Elder Yoder demanding we leave the premises. Frank made a show of trying to decide if he was going to stick around, but without an injured person, he had no case.

I climbed into my van, feeling like a destroyer. I'd let myself get bullied over a sick boy, lost a girl and possibly endangered her, and was completely helpless to change any of the circumstances. Frank started his car and stared at me through his window. I knew he wouldn't drive away unless I let him know I was okay, so I gave him a thumbs up, and a 'Yay' fake smile. He nodded and shifted his car into drive, the tires kicking up dirt as he spun it back onto the road.

With a backfire and a jerk, I slowly followed in my van, my

eyes glued to the forest that stretched along the side of the road.

Where was Mary? And, more importantly, where was Jacob?

———

THE NEXT MORNING, I woke up in my apartment, drained with the feeling of failure. A young girl had asked me for help for her hurting friend. And somehow, in a matter of hours, I'd lost the both of them.

Sighing, I climbed out of bed and wandered into the kitchen. I should make myself something to eat, but I wasn't that hungry, knowing that I'd be lucky to scrounge up peanut butter and jelly from the cupboards at this time before my paycheck. I'd eat at Cecelia's later. She probably wouldn't mind, especially if I did the dishes.

I knew what would make me feel better. Where was my fuzzy bathrobe? I searched for the purple puff of softness and found it in the laundry hamper. Dirty or not, I needed it today. It was my idea of decadence, like finding just that right scent of body wash, or the perfect espresso at a coffee stand. Grandma had gotten me the robe for my twentieth birthday. It had seen better days but still I wore it. There was makeup on one arm from where I'd wiped my eyeshadow brushes, and a few thin patches from the many times through the washing machine. Still, it reminded me of Grandma's hugs and I snuggled into it now.

After tying the belt around my waist, I flopped into the kitchen chair. Sitting on an easel before me was a canvas painted with a background of cerulean blue. Painting was another thing I did for comfort. I grabbed my brush and dipped it into purple acrylic and began painting monster swirls. I added pear green and cadmium yellow and suddenly flowers emerged. A field of grass, blue sky.

I swirled one of the brushes in water. The frustrated feeling had eased, but not enough. I had to find the girl. There was nothing for it.

What had Mary said? That there was a man's farm that Jacob had gotten into trouble on. Could I find it?

Not without my partner in crime. With a smile, I called my best friend, Kari. We'd known each other from high school, but with her being the head cheerleader and me the head library nerd, our common ground back then was about the size of a postage stamp. But adulthood changes a lot of things and it wasn't long after graduation that our close friendship fell into place.

She answered on the first ring. "What do you want? I'm in a PTA meeting," she hissed.

"Want to get out of it? I need some help. Can you meet me at my apartment?"

The phone muffled, but I could still hear her tell someone, "Sorry, it's my kids. The house is flooding. Dishwasher, I guess." Then she was back on the line. "I'm on my way."

I chuckled as I hung up. I could always count on her.

Ten minutes later, my phone rang again.

"I'm downstairs," Kari said. "Need me to come up?"

"Nah. I'm on my way down. You're quite the liar, by the way. I'm impressed."

She harrumphed. "It's one of those sweet skills you gain when married. Gives you the right tone when convincing your husband that the bag of frozen chicken casserole really did take hours to make."

I laughed and locked the door. I found her by the curb, car idling and blinkers on. I opened the passenger door to her scooting school books to the back seat.

"Watch your step. I think there's a chicken nugget on the floor," she warned.

I climbed in with a little trepidation.

"Oh, come on. You go into graveyards for a living. What's a little chicken nugget to you? Now, where are we going?" she asked, glancing into the mirror and shifting into drive. The car jerked forward as I was trying to find my seatbelt. Quickly, I buckled it.

"I need to get to Sunny Acres," I said, feeling a little breathless as she sped through an ancient yellow light that turned red the second we hit the intersection.

"Really? And why is that?" She laid on the horn at the next intersection. "Buddy! It won't get any greener!"

"Err," I knew better than to say anything. She didn't see anything weird about her driving. Her husband was just as aggressive as she was. "I lost somebody. Rather, two somebodies. A young man who was injured and a girl."

She nodded as she considered what I'd said. Her hand left the steering wheel unmanned to tuck a stray blonde curl behind her ear, making me suck in my breath. "How, pray tell, did you lose two people in the middle of Amish country?"

I tightened my seatbelt. "The girl came to get help for the boy. But then we were chased off by one of the Elders. And by the time I came back with the police, everyone had disappeared. But I have an idea of where the girl went. And I need my side-kick to help me find her."

"Side-kick?" Her eyes narrowed. "What are we, super heroes? I'm no Robin, let me tell you."

"No, more like Laverne and Shirley."

"More like Thelma and Louise, you mean," she snorted, stepping on the gas. "Because I have a feeling this little missing person search of yours is not going to end in our favor."

"It's an adventure! When was the last time you'd been on one?" I wheedled a little.

She sighed. "Don't forget. The last time you used the word *adventure*, we ended up at the police department."

"Please. That was ages ago. A lot has changed since then."

"Well, we'll see."

———

WE ARRIVED at the Amish community. I stared out at all the fields. I wasn't sure if I'd find what I was looking for but I remembered Mary had mentioned a tractor and a huge red silo.

Kari was venting about her night of no sleep. "It's been a crazy week. Colby had a science project that he neglected to tell me about until the night before, and Christina had a slumber party. The girls wanted to watch House. A cute cartoon, right? No. At one in the morning, my bedroom door flew open and eight screaming six-year-olds jumped on my bed. Joe was not happy. He'd been having fitful night sleep because he's been keeping an eye out for a bunch of hoodlums doing drug deals in our neighborhood that our HOA has been warning us about. I'm telling you—"

"What's that?" I interrupted.

"What, this?" She pointed to a driveway that had a little makeshift flower stand made from a tent and a table. Painted milk cans lined the front. But that's not what caught my eye.

In the distance was a silo with a red roof. It had to be the one Mary had mentioned.

"Let's go here," I said, pointing to the flower stand.

A young Amish girl manned the stand. She stood as Kari slowed the car down.

I rolled down the window. "Hi, there."

"Afternoon, ma'am." Her face appeared drawn and serious under her black bonnet. She didn't smile at my greeting.

"What beautiful flowers." I admired the bundles. It was rare to see flowers so early in the season, but the yellow bunches of daffodils and purple hyacinth brightened the underside of the tent.

I glanced out into the field. In the distance, I could see men, presumably her father and brothers, tilling the land.

"Do you own all this land?" I asked her.

"Yes ma'am," she answered. My heart twisted at how solemn she was.

"What is going on there?" Kari gestured toward an open barn. Loud sounds of sawing came from it.

The young girl glanced over her shoulder and whispered. "They be making a coffin."

Kari's face fell.

I was equally as surprised. "I'm so sorry," I said, my hand reaching for the seatbelt at my chest and squeezing it. "Someone close to you?"

The girl shifted uncomfortably and then nodded. "But it's important to remember that life comes and life goes, like the weeds thrown into the fire."

I froze, hearing the parable again.

Kari nudged me. "You ready to go?"

I swallowed and nodded. "Again, I'm sorry."

Numbness filled me as I tried to process what the young girl meant. And what was I going to do next?

I rolled up the window as Kari let off the brake. We drove past the plowed field toward the direction of the red silo. I watched for signs of a driveway. The property plat was huge and we seemed to drive for a long time until, finally, we came to a break in the fence. It gave a glimpse to a long driveway that wound through the trees, its ending out of sight.

"What do we do now?" Kari asked, squinting as she studied it.

I looked at her.

She stared back at me. "Looks like they might have dogs. A shotgun. And lots of those pesky *Do Not Trespass* signs." She blinked and I still said nothing, my brain trying to spin up a plan. She sighed. "You really want to go down there?"

"No. You're right. Keep driving," I agreed, grimly.

"You sure? Because we could totally Thelma and Louise the driveway."

"Maybe there's another way. Let's just keep going." Even though the red silo was teasing me, I didn't have a good reason to go knocking on some stranger's door.

Kari crept past the driveway to give me a good chance to change my mind. There were men working in this field as well. I knew some of them had to see us, but they didn't react.

She started speeding up when she saw I wasn't going to stop her. The property's fence seemed to continue forever and the driveway was a good ways off when I saw the pond. I straightened, remembering Mary's story of a tractor that Jacob had gotten stuck in the water, which caused the first fight.

We came up upon an Amish woman walking along the side of the road. Her dark dress made her almost blend into the dirt background, except for the white of her apron and a white head covering.

I turned in my seat as we passed. The woman's face was streaked with tears.

"Can you pull over?" I asked Kari.

She responded so abruptly that my seatbelt locked. I scrambled to unlock it and climbed out.

The woman stopped, her eyes wary.

"I'm sorry," I said, with my hands up. "I'm not trying to scare you. We were driving by and noticed you were upset. Are you okay? Is there anything I can do to help?"

She glanced at the field, but we'd long passed the working men. Her fists clenched tightly to her side and she blinked hard. Then the fight seemed to drain out of her and she wilted before my eyes. I don't think I'd ever seen a more broken woman. Including my own face reflecting in the mirror after Derek died.

I took a step forward. "I'm not going to hurt you. How can I help?"

Kari climbed out of the van, and the woman flinched at the sound of the car door.

"It's okay," I said soothingly. "She just wants to help too."

"There's nothing you can do," the woman said. Her voice was husky from crying.

"Does this have to do with Jacob?" I took a chance and asked.

She jerked at the sound of his name and swiftly looked over her shoulder. Her buttoned boots scraped in the gravel. When she turned back my way, her mouth quivered as if she might burst into tears again.

"What do you know of him?" she whispered. "Are you one of the English he got into trouble with?"

"I ... I saw him yesterday," I stammered, suddenly terrified of her relationship with him and what might have happened.

Her body stiffened as though electrified. "Where did you see him?"

"At the wheelhouse by Sunny Acres. A young girl led me there."

At the words "young girl," the woman burst into tears. Her mouth dropped open as though she were screaming, but no sound came out.

I ran over. "What's wrong? Do you know Mary?"

"She's gone," she gasped.

"Gone?" Cold chills ran down my spine. "Do you think she's hiding? I saw her with her friend."

"Naomi is back, but Mary is still gone. Naomi knows not of where she is. Mary was supposed to be back for milking. She never came home. No one has seen her."

"What's your name?" I asked.

"Rebekah," she said simply.

"Where are you going right now?"

"To the pond."

"Why is that?" I pressed gently.

"Because Mary liked to hide in the back of this property." She bit her lip. "I'm hoping she's there. Maybe something scared her off."

I remembered how Mary had told me about the tractor. Now it occurred to me that it might not have been a story she heard, but something she might have seen first hand.

"Are you allowed in the van? Can we drive together?" I asked.

Rebekah's eyebrows rose in uncertainty.

"Okay. How about if I walk with you? Is that okay?" I asked.

She nodded and the creases under her eyes lessened in relief.

"Kari!" I yelled. "Can you wait here?"

I heard the car door close, and then Kari stuck her hand out the window, giving me a thumbs up.

Rebekah and I continued to walk down the road. Silently, we made our way around the field. Finally, she headed down the ditch and through the fence. I followed. We pushed through the weeds and, up ahead, I could see the pond.

"Mary told me he worked here," I pointed ahead.

"This farm belongs to Mr. Murray. I don't know much about him, other than he's the one who owned the tractor that Jacob lost."

Rebekah walked over to the pond and pointed to the grass. The grass was torn up, possibly from when they pulled out the tractor. There were odd footprints, the muddy tread marks noticeable stamped with a circle and a K.

"How did everyone find out?" I stepped closer to where Rebekah pointed.

"Mary. She went for a walk and saw it happen."

"A walk or...?"

"Perhaps she was hiding in her cave. She liked to go there in the evening after she supped."

With that, she turned and headed up a hill.

CHAPTER 6

The grass was a tangled mess up here on the hill. But I could still faintly see a trail where the grass was parted. Someone had been this way recently.

Rebekah pushed through silently as the weeds grabbed onto her skirt. One briar bush stuck ferociously, and she ripped it free. I winced at the tearing sound but she didn't seem to notice.

I glanced up and could make out a dark mark way up on the hillside. That must be the cave we were aiming for. Birds chirped from the frail branches of the bushes around us.

Rebekah panted and wiped her forehead with the back of her hand, leaving a dirty smudge behind.

"You doing okay?" I asked.

She nodded but I was worried. Her face was an odd color. Cheeks flushed red, but otherwise a gray complexion. My heart squeezed for her as she cast a hopeful gaze up the hillside.

The bushes held tiny buds of promised leaves. I thought maybe they were blueberries, but it had been a long time since anyone had attended them. They grew out from their neat rows and intertwined branches with one another.

We continued up the hill. It was odd how silent everything was, and my breath was loud in my ears. The hillside was steep, with the sun beating on the crown of my head as I watched my footing.

"We're here," Rebekah murmured. She brushed back a large bush that partially blocked the entrance and disappeared inside.

My hope disintegrated at her continued silence. There must be no one in there. Feeling like there was a lead ball in my stomach, I pushed through the branches and crawled after her.

It was a narrow crevasse with barely enough room for me to stand without banging my head on the jagged ceiling. It took a second for my eyes to adjust.

As I dreaded, Mary wasn't there. Rebekah stood with her

hands wringing the front of her skirt. Her knuckles were white from her effort.

"We'll find her," I said, softly touching her elbow. Her eyes filled with tears at my words.

"Maybe she's hiding somewhere else," I suggested. "Maybe she'd been discovered here and has another safe place."

I studied the narrow space for clues. The cave floor was swept clean. Chalk drawings filled an entire wall. A book was in the corner next to a stub of a candle. Crouching, I walked over to read the cover. *Beautiful Thoughts*.

"Do you recognize this?" I asked.

Rebekah shuffled over. After reading it, she picked it up and held it to her chest. "Mine, from my childhood. I wonder where she found it."

She opened it and read the dedication. With a smile, she showed me.

Honestly, I couldn't read the script. When she caught my confused expression, she read out loud.

To my Darling Rebekah. Remember God has you. Momma

She started to close it when I asked her to flip through the pages. Call it a hunch, but I'd seen a pucker in the middle where the pages didn't line up. The book sprung open right to that spot.

The corner had been turned down with a note written in the margin. "I wish I wasn't hiding this secret. Why did Jacob do it?"

The writing stopped there.

Rebekah covered her mouth. A soft sob escaped between her clenched fingers.

I didn't know what to say. I felt like I should do something, but every thought that came to my head was stupid. Things like, "It'll be okay. She's out there somewhere," seemed insane in the face of this woman's fear.

"I'll help you look for her," I finally said, rubbing her arm. "I know people who can help."

At that horrible moment, my cell phone buzzed, causing me to jump. I scrambled it from my pocket, intending to mute it until I saw it was from Kari.

"Hello?"

"Georgie? Where are you? We have friends."

The stress that threaded through her voice was unmistakable. I needed to get back, now.

"On my way," I said. She clicked off, making me feel even more nervous.

"Rebekah," I said gently. "How can I get hold of you?"

Her eyelashes were spiky from tears as she looked at me. She didn't answer.

"I have to go. Someone's down at the road bothering my friend."

She stared in the direction of the road and then back at me, her eyes wild.

"It's okay. She's going to be fine. But how do I get hold of you again?"

Her tongue darted out to lick a very dry, chapped bottom lip. The chapping extended past her actual lip, creating a red shadow below it. And then she seemed to decide. "If you hear from my Mary, go to the milking shed. I work there every day."

I nodded. "Do you want to come back with me?"

Her hands squeezed her apron even tighter and she shook her head.

"I won't make you, and I won't tell anyone you're here," I reassured her. She smiled at me, gratefully. Then I pushed through the bush and headed down the hill. When I glanced back for Rebekah, she was nowhere to be seen.

I didn't have a second to think about that, as now I was skidding on a rock and landing on my butt. I slid a hundred feet in a cloud of dust and rolling rocks. Shakily, I got back to my feet and started down with greater care.

I stumbled around the pond still picking gravel out of my hands. There was Kari's car and a figure of a man. As I walked closer, I could hear Kari say cheerfully, "There she is now."

A beefy, older man leaned outside her window, not in a friendly way of wanting to chat, but threateningly. His index finger was jabbing forward angrily.

I slowed my steps, trying to figure out how to approach this. Do I tell him where I went? What other excuse do I have?

"Hi there," I said, crossing the drainage ditch.

He turned towards me and scowled. "Trampsing about my property, I see." His face was ruddy, with a white line on his forehead from where he normally wore a hat. White wrinkles fanned out against the tanned skin from the corners of his eyes. Was this the Mr. Murray that Rebecca had referred to earlier?

"What are you doing there?" he asked, his voice raspy.

Kari stared at me anxiously.

My first instinct was to lie. I'm kind of ashamed of it, but the flaring of the man's nostrils made me too afraid to confess to searching his property for a young girl.

"I thought we hit an animal. It disappeared into your blueberry bushes. I just wanted to check to make sure it wasn't hurt."

Kari nodded. "Yeah, like I told you, she'd be right back. I told you she had a good reason to go on your property."

He leaned away from the car and crossed his arms. His deep-set eyes glowered at me in suspicion.

Carefully, I sidled past him, watching him for any movements like one would watch a rattlesnake. I had no idea where Rebekah was, but I hoped she was far away from here.

"We're leaving right now. Sorry to trouble you," I said, climbing into the passenger seat.

"And we're out of here," Kari whispered. "I swear that guy's scarier than any email my HOA has sent me." She shifted into gear and stepped on the gas.

Maybe a little too hard. The man jumped back as her back tires spit gravel. He shook his fist as we sped off. And we laughed like two loons out of a movie scene.

CHAPTER 7

By the time I arrived at the bed and breakfast, it was after noon. I had the cheesecake I'd forgotten yesterday still sitting on the passenger seat. I pulled the covering back to sniff it—it seemed okay—and carried it with me into the house.

I couldn't wait to see what kind of lunch Cecelia had whipped up. The woman had a way around the kitchen that even Grandma once grudgingly complimented. The scent of garlic and yeasty bread greeted me at the door making my mouth water. Spaghetti and homemade garlic bread. I could cry, I was so happy.

"Hello!" I hollered as I walked in. Power had been restored at some point, and soft music greeted me. I noticed the curtains weren't quite pulled open in the living room and walked in there to fix it. "Cecelia?" I called.

The B&B was vacant of guests today with some more expected that weekend. I walked into the adjoining dining room just as Cecelia was coming through. She wiped wet hands on the front of her apron.

"There you are, GiGi! I was wondering if you were going to show up today."

"Maybe I can trade you?" I lifted the cheesecake. "Plus a dance for a meal?"

"Ohh, my favorite." She came over and accepted the pan from my hands. "Great timing especially since mine didn't turn out yesterday."

"That's actually why I picked it up. Only there's one thing about it. It's been sitting in my van since yesterday."

She gave it a sniff. "No barbecue smell so I'm sure it's fine." She grinned at me.

I slid off my coat and hung it in the closet. "Everyone leave today?"

"Yes, both the Stevens and Walters. Very pleasant, those two couples. We played pinochle for quite some time yesterday, waiting for the power to come back."

"I'm sorry I didn't stop by again. Yesterday was weird." I hedged, following her into the kitchen. I didn't like keeping secrets, and I knew my aunt was respectful of the Amish.

"I knew something must have happened. Oscar came by at around four looking for you."

"For me?" I was surprised and a bit alarmed. He'd never done that before. "Is he okay?"

"Yes." She lifted a pot lid and stirred the spaghetti sauce. My stomach growled in response. "He mentioned something about you saying you'd bring over a turnover?" She tapped the spoon against the side of the pot.

"Oh." I kind of blushed. Here I was, offering people Cecelia's food. "I did say something to him about that. Hope you don't mind."

"No. Not at all. In fact, I had him over for dinner. He played a round of pinochle with us."

"Really?" Now I was even more surprised. Up until this moment, I would have thought Oscar was the very definition of the word, hermit. "Did he... talk?"

"What? Of course, he did. And he was very pleasant as well. Told us all about his days working in the FBI. A very interesting life, he's led."

"Huh. Well, that's good then. I'm glad to hear it."

"I've always told you he's a nice man."

I smiled. Cecelia certainly had, but then she thought the best of everyone.

"Now it's your turn," she said, going to the cupboard for a strainer. "What's going on with you?"

"Me?" I tried, but there was no use trying to fake it.

She gave me a look.

I sighed. "There's some crazy stuff that happened at Sunny Acres. And I've been pretty much kicked out of there. And today another man nearly kicked me off his property too. I just don't know what to do any more."

"GiGi, it sounds like we need a sit-down." Cecelia arched a brow. "You're making a word salad and I have no clue where to start." She went to the window and, with a struggle with the stiff sill, opened it to let the steam escape. "What's this all about?"

A breeze squeezed through the cracked window, carrying the green scent of a promised spring. I sighed as I dragged out a chair and sat in it.

"Things just don't seem to be working out, no matter how hard I try."

Cecelia reached into the cupboard for two mugs—the blue

speckled ones that were my favorite from childhood. I remember when I'd lost my first tooth. Grandma had brought me here to show Cecelia. The two of them had crooned over me while Cecelia made me a cup of hot cocoa and gave me a cookie.

She reached for the gingersnap bag now and I smiled. Those cookies were as hard as rocks, but she did love to dip them in her tea. She set the bag next to me and then returned with two steaming mugs. Then, with a thin eyebrow raised, she indicated the china bowl filled with tea bags sitting in the center of the lazy Susan.

"Dessert before the meal?" I teased as I searched through the tea. I came up with chamomile. I could use some calming today.

"Sometimes rules are made to be broken." She shrugged. "Now start again from the beginning."

"I...think there's been a crime. Maybe even a murder. It was first presented to me as an accident but right now no one's talking and no one even believes me. I called in Frank and I think even he doesn't believe me. And, to top it off, the girl who originally asked for my help is missing. I don't know if the boy is dead or alive, but I'm presuming dead. Conveniently, he's missing, too. All of this is hush-hush. I don't know how to fix it. I've never been in this position before where I felt so helpless." I sighed.

73

"Never?" Cecelia asked quietly. I knew she was referring to Derek's death, and the aftermath when I got into the argument with the fire marshal.

"Not since then," I admitted. "When Derek died."

"GiGi, I'm going to throw something out there. Is it possible, perhaps, that your feeling of helplessness to prevent Derek's death is spurring your drive in this Amish situation? Because it sounds like you've already done all you can do. The police are involved. The elders at the community are involved. It's really out of your hands."

I bit my lip, considering it. Was this whole heavy feeling of failure really about trying to right the past wrongs with Derek?

"In other words," Cecelia stopped mid-dip of her cookie. "Why are you helping them?"

The answer came like a flash. Maybe the negative emotions were from the past, but the reasons to search for answers were definitely from the here and now. "Because Mary is a sweet girl and she was desperate for help. Something happened to that boy but no one believes me. And now Mary is missing and, besides her poor mother, I seem to be the only one who cares."

Cecelia made a thoughtful "hmmm" as she took a sip of tea.

Just then the front door crashed open and a loud, "Honey, I'm home!" rang through the house.

Frank was here. And in an abnormally chipper mood, it seemed.

"In here!" I yelled, feeling a few butterflies. Frank and I had been in a weird place the last few months. Weird because we'd grown closer than I ever dreamed was possible. Weird because we still didn't exactly have a label. It'd been so long since I dated anyone besides Derek, I wasn't sure if people still labeled things. But, consequently, I was kept a bit off guard, not knowing what to expect. I have to admit, the fear was stopping me from completely diving in.

He came around the corner in his police gear.

"You off, honey?" Cecelia stood up and kissed her grandson on the cheek. "Hmm, need to shave, there."

"Yeah, I'm off." He grabbed me in his arms in an uncharacteristic display of affection. "C'mere. Am I stubbly?" He then proceeded to scratch his cheek against mine, ignoring my squeals.

"Yes! Get off of me!" I yelled, after getting a quick squeeze in.

Cecelia laughed and walked over to the drawer where, after lots of rattling, she pulled out a ladle. She dunked it into the spaghetti sauce and stirred. "Time to dish up, you monsters."

She didn't have to ask me twice. At Cecelia's table, you had clean hands, a rule that was stamped into our minds from a young age. I washed first and then took advantage of Frank's time at the sink to dish up.

"Geez, you act like you haven't eaten all week," he observed sarcastically. I didn't say anything, filling my plate with noodles and topping it with homemade spaghetti sauce and meatballs.

"Left one for you," I said casually, making him jump.

He poked around in the pot. "You better have left me more than one."

"Maybe two," I conceded.

"Shush. Frank, you know I make a panful. There's plenty for everyone. Now one of you better help me with the bread and salad or no dessert for you."

I grinned. What was it about coming home that made you feel like a kid again in so many ways?

At the table, after saying grace and taking a few wonderful bites, I started the conversation. "Frank, I'm really worried."

"About...?"

"That girl. Mary. You should have seen the evil look Elder Yoder gave her when he caught us in the wheelhouse."

"I thought you said she ran into the woods with her friend."

"Yeah. She did. But her mom said she never came home." I took another bite trying to decide how he was going to take the next bit of information. "I went up to her hiding place today."

"Hmm?" He arched an eyebrow.

"Yeah, and she left a cryptic note. Something about how she couldn't believe what Jacob had done and she didn't want to hide it."

"Where was this?" he asked, slicing into the crusty bread.

"Oh, in her hiding place," I repeated.

He paused and stared at me. "I'm not deaf. I'm asking where it was."

I hated it when he didn't let me push him off. Grudgingly, I admitted, "Up in a cave."

He didn't respond, just stared with that weighty solemnity of his that said, "I'm not giving up until you cough up all the info."

Whatever. "At the Murray Farm. There's a cave up the hill at the back of the property. I guess it's where Jacob had a confrontation with a gang of men."

CECEE JAMES

He took a bite of the crusty bread and crunched. I relaxed, thinking I was going to get off easy.

"So, trespassing," he finally eased out.

"What? I—no."

"No?" He tipped his head.

Cecelia watched calmly like she was observing a fencing event. And it was obvious who was losing. My shoulders slumped.

"Okay, so this is the way it was—" I began.

"I knew it," he said, stabbing at a meatball.

"No. Wait."

"Listen, Georgie. I pretty much got chewed out by the captain after Elder Yoder had a little talk with him. No matter what it looks like, we can't go hassling them. Is it possible the original story is true? That some kid got drunk and fell down the stairs and is probably home recovering?"

"What about the fact that Elder Yoder said he had no idea who Mary was?"

"He said he was protecting her, and that she'd been hiding at her best friend's house all night. You need to be careful. He threatened to press charges against you. Harassment."

"I thought they didn't like the police in their business," I grumbled.

Frank exhaled slowly and took another bite of his bread. I figured it was so he didn't have to answer me. Why wasn't he helping me more? I thought I could always rely on him. What was going on? I cut my meatball into fourths, pretty sure I wouldn't be able to swallow over the lump in my throat.

"Anyway, guess who I saw the other day?" Frank turned to Cecelia.

"Who's that, dear?"

His gaze cut to me. "An old work buddy. Colleague, really."

I watched him curiously. Did his hand just go through his hair like he was nervous? I joined in. "An old colleague?" That doesn't sound too bad. "Where did you work with him?"

He rubbed his chin, his stubble making a soft sound against his fingers. "Uh, it's a woman, actually." He shook his head. "From my Army days. She was one of the nurses. Geez, it's been so long."

A prickle of alarm grew in my chest. I didn't like the way this was going, not at all.

Still, it was only an old co-worker. Everyone has friends from the past, right? My mind conjured up a tough battle-weary woman. No make-up. Probably a stern face.

"Are you talking about Jessica?" Cecelia asked. The joy in her voice made the prickle stronger. Who was this Jessica and why was her very name evoking so much emotion from Cecelia?

Frank leaned on his elbow. "Yeah, she's back in town for a while. Wanted to touch base again. She said to tell you hello."

"Oh, that's wonderful. Tell her hi from me as well. We should have a barbecue." Cecelia's pink cheeks filled with more color and she clapped her hands together.

"Uh," I started to feel dumb. "Who's Jessica, exactly?"

Frank glanced in my direction. "She's actually one of the nurses who helped me after I got hurt." He rubbed his chest.

"Oh. That's great."

His eyes narrowed. "What? You're not going to be all weird, are you?"

"What? No. I'm just surprised you didn't mention it to me when she first contacted you."

"I didn't know I needed to let you know whenever a military buddy said hello."

Okay, then. I was done. "You absolutely don't. I look forward to meeting her. Maybe at the barbecue." I have to admit, insecurity made me tack on, "If you want me to come."

"Of course, I want you to come. Geez." He rolled his eyes and shoveled in another bite.

Dinner conversation pretty much died out after that, despite Cecelia's few attempts at resurrecting it. But even Cecelia didn't have the power to stomp down the awkwardness swamping that room.

It was with relief when I finally finished and could start doing the dishes. Frank came over to help me. We washed in silence for a few minutes. I handed him the last plate, but instead of reaching for it, he studied my eyes.

"Hey. We're okay, aren't we?"

I nodded. "Yes, of course, we are."

He smiled and took the plate and finished drying. After a good old fashioned make-up session, I said goodbye and headed home.

But that uneasy feeling stayed with me.

CHAPTER 8

Sleep didn't come easy that night between nightmares about Frank and seeing Mary run away over and over no matter how hard I called. The next morning I threw myself back into what I'd named, "The Amish Chronicles." Something was going on, and I didn't care if no one believed me. Until I talked with Mary myself, I wasn't giving up.

I poured myself some coffee and then reexamined the pictures I'd taken earlier from the wheelhouse. Mentally, I kicked myself. They were so dark! Why didn't I use a flash?

Well, they weren't going to be of use to anyone as they were, so I decided to upload to my computer and play around with them. It only took a few moments until I was lost in my work. My coffee was cold by the time I finished going through the layers and lightening them. But I finally cobbled out a fairly visible shot of the boot on the stairs.

I sipped the coffee and grimaced, then leaned in to study the photograph. The laces were strung along the tread with the tongue of the boot hanging out. Whatever had happened must have been violent. I sighed and scrolled to the next picture, the one with Jacob on the floor. But no matter how I lightened this one, it still wasn't a very clear image.

There *was* something that stood out to me

His left foot was still in a boot. The shot had been taken from above, showing his toes pointed upward. What caught my attention was the fact that the boot had extra metal hooks right at the top and the laces tied tight through them, fully lacing it past his ankle.

A person usually doesn't completely lace one boot and only partially lace the other one. So it stood to reason that both boots had been fully laced. That made it seem very unlikely— even impossible— that Jacob would have slipped out of his boot even if he had tripped.

I examined the first picture again—the boot on the stairs— specifically the laces. Sure enough, they were worn a few inches from the ends, as if they were always laced tight around the top hooks.

I pushed the computer away. Was this scene a setup? Was

Mary or someone else supposed to walk in on him looking that way? But then, why clean it all up later and move Jacob?

The blood was another curiosity. From what I saw of his head wound, it had been devastating, but not open. So where did the blood come from? And why were the drops in the same spot as the boot? How was it possible to lose his boot and hit his head on the same stair tread?

My phone buzzed with a text, distracting me. —**Hey Louise, come help Thelma out. You owe me.**

I groaned. I knew it had to be bad for Kari to invoke the 'owe me' clause. —**What is it?**

She wrote back. —**There was a cancellation today on the school field trip. I got roped into it. So did you. You'll love it, it's a historical tour.**

Oh, no. I bit my lip and typed, —**what ages?**

She ignored the question, typing instead, —**I'm bringing doughnuts!**

Lovely. She was really trying to sweeten me up. That could only mean one thing. The age range was Junior High. The girls were okay, but those teen boys—oh geez.

But what could I do? Gritting my teeth, I typed back—**I love doughnuts.**

Two hours later found me sitting on a bus filled with twelve to fourteen-year-old kids.

I picked a paper airplane made out of a gum wrapper from my hair and said, "I wonder if talking with Mr. Murray would help? Maybe we just got off on the wrong foot. I can see why he was defensive. After all, it seems there was some commotion from a bunch of guys threatening Jacob on his property. And it *was* his tractor that Jacob put in the pond."

"I don't know. I think you should drop it. It's not our culture. I mean, what if Jacob is actually okay? He could be," Kari said. Swaying a bit, she stood and reached into the seat behind her, snatching a straw. "No spit wads on my watch," she said to the kid.

I closed my eyes, remembering the sensation of something hitting my back earlier.

A heavy breath escaped me. I was torn with what to do. Everyone was giving me advice to drop it, but I just couldn't. Maybe I could track down who Jacob hung out with during his Rumspringa. Maybe find the girl that Mary had said he'd kissed. Or try to get back into Mr. Murray's good graces and ask a few questions. Either one of those encounters could help shed light on the situation, but it also meant I was asking people about a possible murder that wasn't even being investigated.

I listened to the chatter of the kids while Kari played on her phone. We were headed to a place fondly known as "Old Towne," a section of Gainesville where the oldest school, church, and government buildings resided. The school and government buildings were simply tourist attractions, but the church was still operating as it had for over a hundred years.

Within fifteen minutes, we made it to Old Towne. That was about all I could stand in the moist air of the teen-sweat scented bus. It made Old Bella seem like a florist shop in comparison.

The bus door opened with a hiss, and I jogged down the stairs, followed by a horde of laughing, teasing, loud kids. Nerves jangled inside me since I had no idea what I was going to do to quiet them down.

I looked to Kari to lead, but she'd stepped back and was staring expectantly at me. Fine. I could see how it was.

I cleared my throat and began, "All right, ladies and gentlemen. If you can just follow me, we'll get this tour going."

For starters, I led the group of teens to the old school. There were framed photographs still hanging on the walls of the small building, most of women in long dresses with high collars, dour expressions and tight buns. Glass cases ran down on either side of the door, containing remnants of days long passed. Peeking inside showed crumbling textbooks, a tarnished bell, and writing implements that were no longer used. Along the back wall was a counter that was covered with colorful brochures of some nearby attractions and information on the history of the school.

The kids filed in, and I answered the usual questions, but most were smart-aleck remarks that I tried to ignore.

After that, we headed to the government building, which was a lot more interesting, at least to me. There were more framed photos and newspapers— this time showing men in wire-rimmed glasses and huge mustaches. There were books and artifacts placed on scattered tables around the room. The main room held a few busts of prominent figureheads, stamped below with brass plaques about their deeds. A few glass cases showed old laws that had been passed and the antiquated forms of punishment for the breaking of said laws.

In the back of the room was a long glass display case exhibiting a scaled down model of the gallows as well as several more miniature examples of forms of punishment. It was always the tourists' favorite aspect of the building.

Naturally, it was the kids' favorite, also.

"Were there witch trials here?" One of the girls asked.

I nodded. "Somewhat. It was nothing as big and severe as Salem, but as with many of the small settlement towns, it definitely occurred. There was a period in the late 1800s when a few women and one man were accused of conspiring with dark sources. They were found guilty of witchcraft and hung."

"Was it the Amish who did it?" another kid asked.

"No. The Amish people came over in the 1700s and settled separately from our society. See, they were trying to get away from Catholic persecution in England but they didn't like the loose beliefs and discipline of the main settlements over here. So they built their own town and lived apart from the 'English' as they call us."

There were nods and raised eyebrows at the information.

"Do they have to obey our government?" asked another girl.

I answered with a shrug. "Yes and no. The government gives them some wiggle room with laws, permits, education, and other things, but they do have parts they have to live by. There's some protection with being a religious sect, so their taxes and education issues are different."

"Do they live the same as they always have?"

"Pretty much. They've made some adjustments to modern living in their own way, but they still do a lot that is reminiscent of the days of settlements."

"What about bathrooms?" It was the girl again.

"They have indoor plumbing but it isn't modern like our own. They don't have electricity so any water for bathing has to be heated by fire. On the other hand, they also have outdoor toilets so they don't have to track dirt or anything inside when they are working on the farm. Not to mention with large families, that makes a lot of people waiting for the bathroom, so it helps to have another alternative."

I fielded a few more questions as we walked over to the church. The stained-glass windows and river rock walls were always a favorite target of photographs. A few kids went inside while I described the history of the old church, including one unfortunate fire.

Then we all climbed back on the bus to return to the school. Kari counted heads while I sat sideways in one of the seats, congratulating myself on a job well-done. I peeked through the crack to the seat behind me, where a boy sat with headphones on.

We met eyes and I asked, "What'd you think? Did you have fun?"

He slid the headphones around his neck. "That Amish stuff was interesting. I met one of them. He stayed with my brother, Dylan."

"Really?" I asked. "When was this?"

"A couple months ago. He was a cool guy. Spoke funny but he was up to try anything."

I straightened in the seat. Was this my chance to learn more about Jacob? "Do you remember his name?"

The kids shrugged. "Yeah, Jacob Dienner. I remembered it because his last name was like dinner. Funny, huh?"

"Very." I nodded. Trying to be casual, I tucked my hair behind my ear and then continued. "Do you know if he had a job? Maybe a girlfriend?"

"Oh, a girlfriend." The kid laughed. "Yeah, he was a little naive. Got the one girl who had a boyfriend."

"A boyfriend? That couldn't have gone over too well."

"Yeah. The guy was actually from Pittsburgh. He came over to my brother's and tried to start trouble. My brother ended kicking Jacob out. I think that's when he returned back to his village."

"Really? Why did your brother kick him out? The boyfriend was too tough?"

"Too tough? He's *the* guy. The one you don't mess with. He drives a blue car with a spoiler. There are rumors he's buried a few bodies."

"Seriously?"

The kid shrugged again. "Who knows. Probably all talk, but my brother said he did put a guy in the hospital. Never did any jail time for it."

I nodded again. "Has your brother had trouble with Jacob or the boyfriend again?"

"Nah, man. We aren't close and I actually haven't talked to him since. Last I heard, my brother got spooked and was talking about reenlisting with the Navy."

I settled back into my seat. There was that word again. The same one Mary had applied to Jacob.

Spooked.

Just then I got a text. It was from Frank, and it read, —**It's official. Jacob's dead.**

CHAPTER 9

I texted back.—**Where are you?**

He wrote. **—Outside the Amish church. You coming?**

I told him I'd be there as soon as possible. After the bus returned to the school, I jumped into the van and headed over there, my mind spinning to be finally given information about Jacob.

I parked in the small dirt parking area at the Amish village center meant for visitors and got out, not sure where to even find Frank. Lucky for me, I didn't have to figure that out. He was standing at the double doors of the church which were propped open. I gave him a tight smile as I walked over.

"I can't believe it." I shook my head. A large Amish man walked in front of me, making me suck in my breath. But it wasn't Elder Yoder.

Frank came down the stairs to meet me, already talking. "Yeah. It appears Jacob is not only dead but already buried."

"What? Really?"

"Funeral was this morning." He cracked his knuckles and stared over my shoulder. I followed his gaze. Naomi, Mary's friend, was walking up to us. She wore a dress in dark brown, her hair covered with a similar material.

I was ecstatic to see her. "Naomi! How are you?" Enthusiasm gushed through me and I mentally told myself to reign it in, especially on such a somber occasion.

"As well as can be. We had the wake for Jacob at his father's house." Her bottom lip quivered but she stiffened her shoulders and drew her chin up.

I frowned. "I'm so sorry. How is Mary?" The last question came out in a rush. I couldn't help myself, so anxious for news of the girl's whereabout.

Naomi seemed about to answer when a black buggy pulled in next to the church with a roar of "Whoa, now" and grinding wagon wheels. Several Amish men hopped out and opened the back. They lifted out several chairs while one of them waved Naomi over.

She nodded and hurried in their direction, making it a few steps before suddenly turning back. The girl winced slightly before saying, "She's... she's fine."

My mouth went dry. She was lying to me, I could tell. Elder Yoder had lied as well. Where was that poor girl?

"Can I talk with her?" I asked softly.

Naomi picked at a thread on her sleeve. "She's working right now."

"Working where?"

"Ask her mother. Over at the milking barn." Her eyes caught mine, looking large and beseeching. "I must go." She continued over to the men.

Frank and I watched her walk away, her boots hidden by her long skirts. He pulled a toothpick from his pocket and stuck it in his mouth.

"So, where we going next?" he asked and switched the toothpick to the other side with his tongue.

"Uh, how do you know I'm going somewhere?"

He looked at me now and his brows lowered over eyes. "Let me think of an Amish way to say this. I didn't fall off the turnip wagon yesterday. I know you, and know how that brain of yours works."

"I have twice the brain as you have," I teased back, the old joke stemming from our childhood. "And I have a good feeling that's not an Amish saying. But yes, you're right. I want to find Mary and make sure she's okay."

"Let's get going then," he said. "I don't have all day."

I rubbed my forehead, not at all sure of where to start looking for a milking barn. Finally, I headed towards a group of women sitting in a circle under a tree, not looking to see if Frank was following me.

"Hello," I waved as I approached. "I do historic tours in town and recently brought a couple of tourists through here a few days ago. I heard I should check out the milking barn. Can you point me in the direction of where that is?"

Several of the women glanced at each other before ducking their heads at the throat clearing of an older lady in the center.

"It's over there," a young woman chimed in. Her words were met with a disapproving glance from the older woman. I swallowed hard, suddenly feeling caught in the middle of a stare down.

Well, you know what they say. Go big or go home. "Uh, do you know if Rebekah works there?"

A murmur of disapproval worked its way around the women's circle. Every bonneted head—some black to indicate they were single, some white to show they were married—bowed over their sewing. The older woman's flinty stare was more than adequate to let me know there would be no more talking.

I thanked them and backed away.

"Always with the silver tongue," Frank said, suddenly appearing at my elbow.

"Where were you when I needed you?" I grumbled, heading in the direction of the barn.

"I figured you'd get more information from the women if I stayed out of sight." He snorted, walking next to me. "Apparently, I was wrong."

If we'd been anywhere else I would have socked him on the arm. But out of respect for the Amish, I bit my tongue and reigned in every reaction. He must have seen he'd hit a nerve because he covered quickly, "Hey, I'm just kidding. Geez. So sensitive lately."

I sent him a stiff smile and lengthened my steps. As I got

closer to the barn, the smell of cow manure made my nose wrinkle.

"Hey." Frank tapped my arm. "You go on ahead. I'm going to wait here." He pointed to the corner of the building.

I nodded and continued over to where I saw a side door open. Taking a deep breath to strengthen my courage, I walked inside.

Several doors and side hatches were open, allowing the sunlight to brighten the majority of the dark interior. Women sat in the stalls, one per cow, milking them. Quiet chatter filled the air.

I glanced around but didn't see Rebekah or Mary, and my heart sank. I walked down the row, giving smiles and nods to the girls on stools. It was with relief when, near the end, I spotted the girl's mother.

I walked over to her and hesitantly reached out to pat the cow. "Rebekah, how are you?"

The woman glanced up before resuming her work. I raised my eyebrows, wondering if I was getting a tiny taste of being shunned.

I tried again. "I was hoping to find Mary here, as well."

Rebekah ducked her head tighter against the side of the cow. We waited that way for a few minutes, the steady hiss, hiss, hitting the metal bucket. I wondered if she would ever answer. Finally, she stared meekly at me and gave me a slight shake of her head.

With the drawn lines on her face and dark circles under her eyes, I assumed she was answering my unasked question on if she knew where her daughter was. She stood then and drew her skirt to the side to see the stool. Picking it up, she said in a matter-of-fact tone, "I have some news. We've had someone come forward."

I frowned but said nothing. Rebekah set the stool against a wall and grabbed the bucket of milk.

"This way," she nodded.

Together, we walked out the side door. Frank saw us and straightened from where he'd been leaning against the wall, but he didn't follow. We walked to another barn, a white one with large windows.

"This morning Elder Yoder let us know that Brother Matthew had confessed to harming Jacob. He had wished Jacob unwell and got into a confrontation in the wheelhouse. Apparently, Brother Matthew was angry with Jacob since Jacob had met an English girl at Rumspringa."

I bit my cheek as I tried to process this new information. "Are you saying Matthew killed Jacob by pushing him down the stairs?" This was the first time Jacob's death was being presented as something other than a drunken accident.

"We are not privy to that information."

What was this? "So Matthew may not have actually killed Jacob?"

Her voice was monotone. "That's between him and the bishop. What we do know is that he's been shunned for a few months and the bishop will be discussing the issue with some of the nearby communities on what should be done beyond that." Rebekah slowed her steps and made her words even more deliberate. "The community is satisfied because it means the issue is over." She gave me a side-eye, and suddenly I was under the impression she was wondering if I was buying what she was selling.

"Why are you telling me this?" I asked.

She jolted forward and the pail jogged against her leg, sloshing milk up the sides of the pail. "Elder Yoder expressed to me that, should I see you again, I needed to inform you." Her chest shook with a breath. "And then I'm not to speak with you again."

I froze in my steps. "But what about Mary? Where is she?"

Her eyes welled with tears and her lips pressed together. "I must go," she whispered and disappeared into the white barn.

I stood outside the doors, unsure of what to do. I spun to look for Frank, breathing in relief when I saw him by an apple tree.

"Well," he asked, toothpick clenched between his teeth. "What did you learn?"

Bitterness flowed through me. "I learned that people can get away with murder by being protected with antiquated laws."

CHAPTER 10

Frank walked with me to my van and opened the door. I raised an eyebrow, not sure if he was being chivalrous or if he was assuring himself that I'd leave the premises without getting into any more trouble.

"I'm sorry, Georgie," he said. And he did look sorry, with his mouth turned down and that cute wrinkle he got in his forehead when he was sad. He leaned in to kiss me, but afterwards, his eyes were serious as he pulled away. "Listen, you need to leave this alone now. All we have, at best, is a boy who fell down the stairs and died of his injuries. At this point, the Gainesville police department isn't going to get involved. And that confession is useless. Holding ill-feelings against someone doesn't exactly hold a lot of water with the sheriff's department." He sighed. "I know you're convinced something else happened, but it's time to get back to your own life. Maybe help Oscar some more. You know that old man always has something around his house that needs to be fixed."

I rolled my eyes but managed to keep the sarcasm out of my voice. "Thanks for your help, Frank."

He grunted. "Well, that's just great. You're using your extra polite voice with me. Means you're super angry."

"I'm irritated," I confessed.

"Listen, I get that this feels personal—"

"It is personal!" I interrupted. "I found the boy before he was dead. And a girl who was desperate for my help has gone missing."

"Hold up. Let's get back to the facts. Do you know for sure the girl is still missing?"

"Well, I—yes."

"How? Did you talk to her mother?"

I thought of Rebekah and felt uncomfortable. "Yes."

"And she said the girl is missing?"

The creeping feeling grew. "Not in those exact words."

"Not in those exact words? What exact words did she use?"

I clenched the steering wheel as the irritating feeling grew. "Her...eyes," I reluctantly answered.

He sighed. "Georgie, did you even ask her?"

"I did, and she didn't answer. She was too scared. She told me about Matthew."

"And that's the one she said was confessing to unkind thoughts?" Frank groaned and covered his face with one enormous hand like he used to do as a kid when exasperated. His palm muffled his words, but I still heard, "Like I said. There's nothing here. I can't go to my chief with your intuition."

"Frank Wagner," I shouted. "How dare you make it seem like my gut feeling is something to be made fun of!"

He held his hands up in defense. "Now, hold your horses. I never said I didn't believe it. I'm saying what it would sound like to the chief if I pushed to continue the investigation."

My irritation had grown to the point I was now shaking. I was so mad. Trying to keep my words reigned tight, I gritted out, "I'll talk with you later."

He stepped back from the van. "Remember you need to—" I shut the door, cutting him off. I needed to get out of there.

Frank gave me a look, and I mouthed "Sorry," knowing how Frank liked to get in the last word. But if I talked to him now I wasn't so sure how that conversation was going to end. I needed a minute to calm down.

He backed away and waved, and I nodded in response before glancing over my shoulder and throwing the van in reverse. *Okay. Breathe.*

Despite how Frank made it sound, I had seen Rebekah's eyes. They were filled with fear. Those weren't the eyes of a mother who knew where her young daughter was. They were the eyes of someone being threatened.

Was Mary being held captive? Why threaten Rebekah? I remember Rebekah saying she was instructed to tell me that someone had confessed. How did Elder Yoder know I'd be back, and why would he want me to drop it?

After today's reception, I wasn't so sure I would be welcome at the Amish village. I needed to think of another way to keep investigating.

I thought back to the kid on the bus. He'd said that his brother had Jacob as a roommate. What was his name again? I'd gotten the kid's last name from Kari and texted it to myself so I wouldn't forget. At the stop sign, I checked my messages. Immediately, a notification showed up from Frank, probably lecturing me some more. I ignored it and went to the one I'd sent myself.

Dylan Weston. I typed the name into the search engine and

came up with a physical address. I smiled grimly at the, "And, for just 2.99 more, you can access his phone number!" and plugged the address into my GPS.

Twenty minutes later, I was driving in the outskirts of the next town over, searching through the apartment's complicated parking lot for a building V. The complex place was huge and every parking spot filled, even the ones reserved for guests. Finally, I found it and, after checking the address again, confirmed he lived in apartment 211. I skirted around the building, hunting for 211.

There it is. I shifted the van into park behind some cars already filling the stalls. My van was blocking part of the parking lot but there was nothing I could do. Other cars would just have to go around me.

There were two doors on each landing, with 211 being on the second floor. I ran up the flights of stairs and knocked on the door.

Children's laughter rang through the parking lot from across the complex. A dog barked and a car revved up. But there was no noise behind the closed apartment door.

I knocked again, harder this time.

This time I got a response, but not what I was expecting. The second door on the landing opened up, with a sleepy-looking woman stumbling out to lean against the frame.

"You looking for Dylan?" she asked. Mascara smeared under her eyes.

"Yeah. You know where he is?"

"Probably at work. Down at the Cash and Carry." With that, she ducked back inside, and the door slammed shut.

CHAPTER 11

I drove through the Vanilla Bean espresso stand, needing a pick-me-up as I tried to decide how weird it would be for me to corner Dylan at the grocery store. I rolled down my window to make my order but it only took two rotations to realize it was stuck. Old Bella was at it again. I was half-laughing as I was forced to open the door, making the barista blink. Without giving an explanation, I ordered, paid, and accepted the steaming cup with much gratitude.

I sipped my espresso, feeling a headache in the back of my eyes. I rolled my neck as ideas tumbled in my head. Honestly, I didn't have the slightest clue as to what I would say to Dylan.

Still, the insecurity didn't stop me, and a few minutes later, I was turning into Cash and Carry parking lot. I studied the building, watching shoppers go in and out. Finally, after one more swig of the coffee, I got out. Words worked through my brain as I practiced my introduction to Dylan while I walked through the parking lot and into the store.

My attention was caught when I entered by a series of pictures inside the doorway. In a row above pinned homemade advertisements for babysitting and yard work were the employee pictures. February's employee of the month was a teenage girl with a thin-lipped grin that made me suspect she was hiding braces behind that smile. In the center of the row, with two chins and a very tight collar, was the smiling face of the owner. My blood nearly ran cold when I realized I'd seen him before. He was the one outside Kari's car the day I met Rebekah.

Mr. Murray.

I silently groaned and nearly left, my courage draining away like water through a hose. I definitely wasn't looking forward to seeing him again. But, with a deep breath and a straightened spine, I finally forced myself toward the check stands and looked for the manager. Not seeing one, I went up to one of the checkers.

"Excuse me," I said when I'd caught her attention. "You think you could call the manager for me?"

She nodded, dragging a package of refrigerated cookie dough over the scanner with a beep. "Just one second, ma'am."

I moved a few feet from the stand in an attempt to give the customer she was helping some privacy. The checker reached for the phone while waiting for the customer to slide her card.

Her voice carried over the store, calling the manager to the front. I pointed to the flower arrangements to show her where I'd be waiting.

Several minutes later, a man wearing a red vest strode toward the checker where she jerked her thumb in my direction. His gaze followed and I lifted my hand. He flashed me a smile, the kind that I myself was an expert at giving when it came to helping the bed and breakfast customers, and headed over.

"How can I help you?" he asked when he reached me. His hand smoothed over the top of his head, highlighting how the hair was receding but still long in the back.

"I'm looking for a young man named Dylan. I heard he works here?"

"Dylan Weston? Yeah, I know him. He left about three weeks ago with that Amish kid he convinced me to give a job to." He shook his head. "It's always bad news to hire an employee's friend. Lesson learned."

"Oh, Was his friend's name Jacob Dienner?"

"Yeah." His eyes squinted in suspicion. "I thought you wanted to know about Dylan?"

"Well, both, actually. Just trying to track down some job references." I hedged with the job reference part.

"That Jacob kid was polite, a quick worker. I remember him buying a set of kid paints, you know those watercolor sets we have on aisle three? I thought it was a funny thing for someone his age to get, but he said it was for a kid he knew back in his village. Then he put his finger over his mouth like it was hush-hush." The manager laughed. "I guess those things are frowned on there. Anyway, there was one incident though." His brow creased. "Something with the owner."

"Can I ask what happened?"

He shrugged. "You'd have to ask him."

I thanked him for his time and started for the front doors. On my way out, I studied Mr. Murray's picture again.

This was getting more and more curious. Both boys quit their jobs at the same time. And then there was the incident with the owner. I didn't know if it was the accident with the tractor or if the manager was referring to something else, but I was on my way to find out.

A few minutes later, I was back on the road and headed toward the Murray's farm. I was beyond nervous and, being so close to my destination, I barely had time to get my thoughts organized before I was pulling down the long driveway. I swallowed hard, my nerves getting to me. My imagination brought up his angry face and tried to convince me there could be nearly anything at the other end of the driveway, including a haunted barn filled with hanging scythes. I shook it off and gripped the steering wheel tighter.

It turned out to be a beautiful house. The home sported a fresh coat of white paint and the quintessential red silo could be seen in the back. Several well-pruned trees and shrubs decorated the yard with the fence cutting off to the right and making a loop around the back to connect at the front of the yard again. The rest of the vast property disappeared in rolling hills that were dotted green with new spring season life.

I parked the van and got out, trying to keep calm as I walked up the steps to the front door. I wiped my hands on my pants and knocked. As I waited, I tried not to appear like I was peeking through one of the door's many glass panes. There was no answer. I was about to knock a second time when I finally heard the approaching steps. Coming toward me was the older, heavy-set gentleman, the same one I'd met earlier under a less than satisfactory situation. Today, he was wearing blue jeans and a light blue shirt, with a shock of white hair sticking out from under a straw hat.

If I hadn't seen him before, I'd have pegged him as unassuming and even a bit adorable in an old farmer guy way, and not at all the business mogul of a big grocery store.

He opened the door. "Can I help you?"

I smiled. "Hello. My name's Georgie. I was wondering if you had a few minutes this morning?"

"What about?" He was suspicious but not rude.

"I'm trying to do some research on the Amish, for a tour that I do for the Baker Street Bed and Breakfast. I have a couple questions."

His brow rumpled and he stared at me harder. "Wait a minute. I know you. You're that lady looking for a dead animal on my property. What are you doing back here?"

CHAPTER 12

*H*is statement was exactly what I'd feared. I swallowed hard. "Well, you see—"

Mr. Murray scowled. But popping up behind him was a woman. Her eyes were anxious but her face was kind.

"Let her in, Jerry" she scolded her husband. "That's not how we treat visitors around here."

He moved back from the door, grumbling.

"Come in, please." The woman opened the door fully. A light breeze swept past and ruffled a few wisps of gray hair that had escaped her long braid. "Now what was it you were saying? You do a tour for that bed and breakfast? Cecelia Wagner owns that, doesn't she?"

I nodded as gratefulness flushed warmth through my chest. "Yes. Exactly."

"Oh, I go to church with her. Would you like some lemonade? I make it myself."

"Absolutely, I would," I accepted and walked in.

The entryway was cozy, with exposed beams contrasting against the white paint of the ceiling. A warm cinnamon scent filled my nose.

"We don't have many visitors now-a-days. Not since the kids moved," Mrs. Murray continued.

"Oh really? Where did your kids move to?" I asked.

"One's down in Texas doing ranching. The other moved clear out to Washington state to work at Boeing."

"Aww, that must be hard having them so far away."

Mrs. Murray led me through the house, with Mr. Murray shambling behind us. I was a little concerned of what he thought of me but he grabbed the glasses from the cupboard while his wife fetched the pitcher of lemonade from the fridge. The décor was all hardwood, hunting trophies, and plaid, very clean and well kept.

She led us through a pair of French doors that opened out onto the back porch. Mr. Murray set the glasses on a wooden picnic table, took the pitcher from his wife, and poured the lemonade.

I waited as both Murrays took seats across from my own and then took a sip. "Very good. And what a beautiful table!"

Mr. Murray seemed more relaxed. He rubbed his hand along the wood. "I got this picnic table from the Amish. In fact, they help me a lot around here."

Mrs. Murray nodded in agreement.

Her husband continued. "The old barn was in awful shape when my sons went away to college, so they helped me repair that. And, every year, a few of the young men come over and help with the fields in exchange for some of the crops. Honestly, I couldn't ask for better neighbors."

I smiled. I had painted a very wrong picture of the old man and was beginning to feel like a horrible person for even thinking such a thing.

"So how can we help you?" Mrs. Murray asked, folding her hands neatly before her.

"Well, I'm trying to get more educated about their Rumspringa. Where they leave the real world for a season? I heard you recently had an Amish employee during his Rumspringa. Could you tell me what that was like?"

Mr. Murray's eyebrow lifted at the word, employee. "You heard that?"

Was I losing him or interesting him? I couldn't tell. "Yes. Actually, I have mutual friends with him. Jacob Dienner, wasn't that his name? The recent news about him has been especially sad."

"Oh really? I hadn't heard," he said.

"Yes, he actually passed away a few days ago." I held my breath, hoping that information wasn't going to close the door between us, both figuratively and literally.

Mr. Murray sucked in a breath, seeming very surprised. He shot a glance at his wife and clenched his hand.

"What happened?" he asked.

I wasn't ready to put all my cards on the table. "I'm not sure, exactly. It seems he may have had a troubled last few weeks. I actually heard there was some mishap here. Jacob drove your tractor into a pond?"

He shook his head sadly. "Yeah, that was something awful. Didn't take Jacob for someone who'd make a mistake like that. He seemed to have a natural talent for mechanics. He and his friend, Dylan quit the Cash and Carry the next day. I heard Dylan's returned to the Navy. Haven't heard anything about Jacob." He looked sick. "Now I know why."

"Do you know what happened with the tractor? How it ended up in the pond?" I took another sip, my tongue rolling over the sour-sweetness.

"Nope. Just that the horn started blaring and I raced down there to see what the ruckus was about. Lucky I was home. Or maybe not so lucky, since all I got was a front row seat to watching my tractor sink in yards of muck. Jacob was real shook up, pale as new milk. I remember him thanking me over and over for coming down. Of course, I came running after hearing the horn blaring like that. Anyone would. I did get hold of one of the Brothers and they brought a crew to help pull the tractor out." He looked at me curiously. "How did you hear about it?"

"Well," I licked my bottom lip. "I heard there was something that happened from your store manager, but the actual story was told to me by one of Jacob's friends. A girl named Mary. Have you ever seen her?"

"You mean the lil' bit who was in love with Jacob?"

My eyes popped open a bit at that. "Are we talking about the same person? She's an Amish girl," I said, trying to clarify.

"Yeah. Cute little thing. I'd always see her black bonnet popping around behind a blueberry bush. Puppy love, I'm guessing. She was constantly watching him. One time, she brought him a picnic basket."

"What do you think he thought of her? Did he return her affection?"

Mr. Murray shook his head. "At first I thought she was his little sister. I asked him one day if she was, and he said no— just an old family friend. I never paid her no mind to being on my property, figured it was harmless."

I rubbed my chin, trying to pull back the memory of having a crush on the band leader in high school. I'll be the first to admit, I fit into the nerdy crowd. But that infatuation had been strong. Had Mary acted like someone in love?

"So you think Mary had a crush on Jacob," I reiterated.

"Something like it. She was here a lot, playing in the pond. I think she might even have a club house."

I nodded and drew my finger back and forth through the condensation on the side of my cup. So the cave wasn't unknown to him.

"But lately, I've been particularly sensitive to people coming on my property. Specifically after the fight."

That perked my interest. "Fight?"

"That day of the tractor incident a crew of boys drove up in my field. Turfed it. I ran out there to see five or six of them screaming at Jacob."

"What? Are you serious?" I gasped.

Mrs. Murray butted in then, her lips pursed. "Dang right, he's serious. He had to bring out his shotgun. They scattered pretty quick then."

CHAPTER 13

The conversation with the married couple went on for almost an hour longer. It was interesting to learn about their interactions with the Amish. And everything I was hearing seemed to prove that the Murrays had good relations with their Amish neighbors.

After the last sip of lemonade, I thanked the couple and said my goodbyes. We left Mrs. Murray clearing the table as Mr. Murray walked me to the front door. He followed me outside, grabbing a rake leaning against the house as he went.

"Mr. Murray, would you object to me checking out the pond area?"

He raised an eyebrow and leaned on the rake. "Something you're looking for?"

I blushed. "Yes, actually Mary. She's been missing since Jacob died."

He hummed and pushed the brow of his straw hat up. "You think she's grieving up in that cave, maybe?"

"I don't think it could hurt to check. Would that be okay?"

Mr. Murray nodded. "But you be careful up there, okay? Don't need another missing person."

"Absolutely." I smiled. "Thanks so much for the lemonade and the talk. It really helped."

As I walked around the side to my van, I noticed a pile of plumbing supplies, including a pile of old, dirty metal pipes and a pile of clean synthetic looking ones, were stacked and strapped on.

"Are you doing some water work out here?"

"Trying to get the irrigation going by the pond. Always having to do upkeep on a place like this."

I nodded, understanding. Just trying to help Oscar with his repairs was a big job. And it wasn't even my place.

As I pulled out of the driveway, I looked back in the rearview mirror at the pile of pipes. My internal wheels were spinning like crazy. I really wished I could talk with Frank, but he'd just push me off again. Sighing, I put on my blinker and turned to drive down Murray's fence line.

Several acres later, I parked in the place where I'd first spotted Rebekah and stared out to the pond. So, sometime recently, Jacob nearly got jumped out here by a gang, the same day he accidentally drove the tractor into the pond. And right after that, he ended his Rumspringa and returned to the Amish. Interesting. Very interesting.

I walked out into the field toward the water, the ground turning marshy the closer I got. It must have rained overnight because the tracks from the tractor being dragged out had turned into mud puddles. And there were those footprints again. I studied them, confused. They all were of the same print. Who danced around in circles like that? But they seemed to be of different sizes. Was it just the rain that had made them look that way?

And how had the tractor ended up in the pond? I walked around the edge of the water, pushing aside cattails and tall grasses, wondering what Jacob had been thinking.

At first, it seemed like there was an obvious explanation. Jacob, as a young Amish man, wouldn't have known how to work a gas engine. But Mr. Murray had clearly said Jacob was good with mechanics and seemed to have a natural knack for it.

Was it possible he would have purposely driven the tractor into the water?

As I walked, I slowly began to comb over the area. The grass was thick and yellow from winter, making it hard to see anything other than a stack of pipes piled to one side from the irrigation project. I really felt like I was looking for a hypothetical needle in a haystack. But, since I was here, I might as well see what I could find. I started to search in a more orderly manner by walking in zig-zags down one side and up the other, hunting for anything that stuck out— a gum wrapper, a cigarette pack, a piece of cloth, anything that could tell me something.

In the end, my walk didn't provide much. I shivered as the temperature dropped. The sun had started to fade toward the horizon and the shadows grew longer. I needed to get up to the cave soon if I still wanted to have any daylight left.

Just as I was about to give up, there was a glint. Brief but bright enough to give me hope. I bent down and delicately peeled back the faded stalks. There it was. A small piece of plastic.

I reached into my pocket and pulled out a tissue. Using it, I picked up the dark piece of plastic. It was smooth on all but one side. I squinted at it in confusion, before wrapping it up and putting it in my pocket. It could be nothing or everything.

With that find, I called my search to a halt. The sun was nearly down and I needed to get up the hill.

After a minute, I found the thin reedy path through the tall grasses that led upward. My heart squeezed as I remembered Rebekah pushing through it with a desperate expression of hope that her daughter had been waiting in the cave. And the horrible way her face had fallen when she discovered the space was empty.

As I waded through the grass, I had hope that I'd have a different result. The cave seemed quiet as I approached, and on my way, I noticed something I'd missed the first time. Some more of those same boot prints with a weird jagged-knob pattern and a circle around a letter K.

I pushed through the bushes and entered the cave. Inside was cold and dark and felt unvisited, making my heart sink. A quick glance proved that the poem book was also missing. I hoped Rebekah had taken it with her. All that remained was the waxy candle remnant and the chalk drawings on the wall.

I stared at them for a minute. Reds. Blues. Greens.

Wait a minute. I rubbed the corner of a picture with my thumb and looked at it. It didn't rub away. It wasn't chalk. It had to be some type of paint.

I spun around. But where was the paint or paintbrush? They had to be around here somewhere.

The floor was clean swept with a roughly-fashioned broom made from ferns and straw sitting in the corner. A smooth rock that had been used as a stool was the only other item.

I stared hard at the candle, noting grease marks in the dirt from the excess wax. A quick study of the rest of the floor showed the same dime-size circles near the back of the cave. I hurried over there and knelt down.

Crumbled pieces of rock were strewn along the wall. I lifted a few but nothing was concealed. Leaning back on my heels, I scrutinized the wall. There was one thick fissure about the width of a pencil. I flashed my light from my cell phone into it but didn't see anything. Gently, I reached my finger inside to feel around.

With a crack that startled me, a ten inch piece of the front of the wall came off. It had been resting on a lip and fitted back into place perfectly. Behind it was a pallet of paint and a paintbrush.

And something else.

CHAPTER 14

*E*xcitement flooded me as I reached into the pocket in the wall that I'd just uncovered and pulled out a torn piece of paper. My hands trembled as I unfolded it.

It was crudely written with what appeared to be ash from a matchstick. *Jacob! Help me. The fat English man is here. He's walking up to the cave.*

I stared at her hastily scrawled words, barely able to grasp her terror at feeling trapped, watching a man walk to her hiding place. She must have hoped Jacob would look here. But did she really think Jacob would be back after his injury? And how would he know about this place?

After setting the paper down, I pulled out the paint set. It was cheap, and I bet it was the one that Jacob had bought. Mary must have been the kid Jacob was referring to when he was talking to the manager.

I examined the outside of the rock opening, this time discovering multiple score marks that looked like they'd been made by a knife. *I bet he made this hidey-hole for her to put her paints in.* I peeked in the hole again, using the light from my phone.

In the very back was what looked like a tube. I reached into my pocket for the same piece of tissue and then folded it around the object and pulled it out.

It was a roll of money, held tight with a rubber band. Stuck in the band was a plastic bag. Tiny. The size of a stamp. It was empty but my stomach clenched inside of me. I'd seen that type of bag before and knew it was to hold drugs.

Mary? I rejected the idea before it had fully formed. No, Mary wasn't a drug user. This had to be Jacob's.

I leaned back on my heels, the money heavy in my hand. I needed to find someone that Jacob interacted with outside his Amish community. Maybe that girl that Jacob kissed. Maybe she could give me some insight as to who he was in the outside world. He was a quandary for sure. Bought his little admirer paints but then hid his blood money in her cave.

I slipped the money into my pocket and left the cave. Carefully, I climbed back down the hill, trying not to slide. I'd stayed up there too long, and it was dusky dark. Carefully, I trekked back to my van. The money burdened me so much I'd almost forgotten about the piece of black plastic in my pocket.

Once in the van, I called Cecelia to see if she needed me to come by tonight.

"Not tonight. In fact, I didn't even make dinner," she admitted.

"Really?" I was surprised.

"Just leftovers for me. Frank called to say he was having dinner out as well. But you're welcome to come by here and help yourself if you'd like."

I was disappointed not to get a chance to see him. It sure would have been helpful to show him the money. I wonder who he had plans with. My chest tightened as Jessica popped into my mind.

"GiGi? You okay?"

Her words jerked me back. "No, I think I'm just going to grab a bowl of cereal for dinner. I'll come by tomorrow, maybe."

"Cereal. Just like when you were a kid, I swear," she said dryly.

I laughed, not feeling it, and we said goodbye.

Back at my apartment, I headed to my bedroom and pulled out the money and plastic with the tissue. I set them on the dresser and then grabbed fresh clothes and headed to the shower. As the warm spray washed away the physical and mental grime, I turned the clues over in my head.

So now I knew why someone would want an Amish boy to die. Drugs. Money. Possibly both. Then there was the girl he kissed. It was a long shot, but she could be a link if her boyfriend was jealous enough. But over a kiss? I shook my head. There had to be something I was missing.

After the shower, I examined the black plastic next to the money. The plastic was rounded and looked to be the corner of something. I started to take a photo to add to my growing album of "Amish Crime Pictures" when the phone fell out of my hand. It landed on the dresser and the shape of the piece of plastic clarified.

It was the corner of a cell phone. I lifted the phone and took the picture and then flipped the plastic over with the tissue to take another one.

Squinting, I leaned closer. The break was sharp and clean, the color wasn't faded. It had broken off recently. In truth, I figured someone helping Mr. Murray—maybe bringing down the pipes—could have dropped his phone, but I doubted it would break hitting the soft ground. But it *would* break if it was hit by something hard. Like during a struggle.

Immediately that goose egg Jacob had on his head came to mind.

"You aren't getting away with it. I'm closing in on you," I whispered. "And I'm going to find Mary, too."

CHAPTER 15

The next morning, I left my apartment and headed to Coffeelotta, one of my favorite coffee shops. Earlier I'd texted Frank about the things I'd found, and he'd said that he would be there this morning and to swing by and drop them off.

I had odd nervous squirreliness in my guts. Even though it'd only been since yesterday, it felt like it'd been a while since we'd actually had time to sit down and talk. And I'd been so irritated the last time I'd seen him.

The van sputtered and I groaned when I noticed the gas gauge. Ugh, almost out of gas. I tapped the gauge hoping it was a fluke, and Old Bella belched out a black cloud seemingly in response. Great.

Come on baby, you can do it. The station was just six blocks ahead, but past the coffee shop.

As I passed the Coffeelotta, I saw Frank's cop car was already there. My heart fluttered with joy as I looked for him in the cafe's windows.

I saw him alright. There was Frank sitting in a window booth. But seated across from him was a beautiful brunette.

It was as if ice water had been dumped down my spine. The woman had gorgeous skin, exotic looks, and silky hair. I'd even bet her nails were painted. I looked at my own, half-covered in blue and red from painting last night, and curled them under the steering wheel.

I swallowed and hoped they wouldn't see me sputter by.

"Come on, Bella," I whispered through gritted teeth. "Be discreet."

Was that Jessica?

I was so consumed with the thought that it could be her, I nearly passed the gas station, and it was only Old Bella's cough that reminded me.

"Crap!" I said, jerking the wheel to pull into the station.

I pulled up to the pump, unscrewed the cap and jammed the nozzle in. Nervously, I started scraping the paint off my thumbnail, glancing over at the attached convenience store. Should I use the restroom to try and clean up?

No, I'm not going to change who I am. I squared my shoulders in determination. I've been through a lot. I'm not going to let some brunette tart—okay, gorgeous brunette tart—intimidate me.

I paid for the gas and minutes later, I pulled into the Coffeelotta parking lot. A quick glance at the cars parked in front showed a brand new Honda. Ugh. It was probably hers.

Trying to shrug off any weird feelings—that wasn't jealousy, was it?—I parked the van and strode inside.

Shoulders back, feeling confident, I let out a deep breath as I approached their table.

The two of them didn't see me coming. Frank had his head back in a laugh.

I stopped short. That laugh nearly undid me. When had I ever seen him laugh like that? I touched my short hair and tucked it behind my ear. Now I felt insecure, frumpy.

The woman looked up and her eyes caught mine. I saw her lean to murmur something to Frank. Her hand briefly touched Frank's, making fire race through my veins.

He glanced over his shoulder and waved at me. "Come on,

slowpoke. Come meet Jessica." He slid over in the booth to make space.

"Hi," I said as I sat down. She smiled and extended a hand to shake mine.

Darn, I was right about the manicure. She gave my nails an odd glance.

"Oh, do you paint?" she asked. I really wanted to think her voice held a tinge of judgment, but it didn't at all. She sounded interested.

"Oh, I just play around. Different landscapes and things." I smiled, trying to grab my mojo.

"Don't let her downplay it. She's an amazing artist." Frank nudged my shoulder. It was sweet but a little brotherly. I was confused as to where to go with that.

"Anyway," Frank continued, "Jessica was in the area so she stopped for a coffee."

"Right," she said, a little abruptly, I thought. "I'm just going to head out."

"Okay. Nice to meet you," I said.

"No, stay. Georgie's only here for a minute." Frank said. Then, turning to me, "So, what did you want to show me?"

Was he trying to get rid of me? Trying to squash the

insecurity, I passed over a plastic bag with the corner of the case, and the stamp-sized bag in it.

"What's this?" he asked, lifting over to the window to examine it in the light.

"I found it."

"I see that. I figured it didn't fall from the sky like sparkly pixie dust."

"Haha," I said dryly. Now for the tricky part. "I—uh— was trying to meet a friend and stumbled across it."

He set the bag down with a sigh and took a long slurp of coffee. I waited for his reaction. He was delaying, so I knew it was going to be a good one.

"Try again, Sherlock. Your story is about as honest as a purple chicken."

I bit my lip, then glanced at Jessica. This was going to be embarrassing. "I was looking for Mary, remember her? I went to a place she liked to hang out and discovered this. And something more."

I eyed Jessica and then slid over the money roll. Frank whistled through his teeth.

"Well now," Jessica said in a purr. "Isn't that something?"

Frank raised an eyebrow. "Where did you say you found this?"

"On Mr. Murray's land."

He ever so slowly raised an eyebrow. "And why were you there?"

"To, um..." My gaze cut to Jessica who had started to smirk.

"She was there to sell Girl Scout cookies, what else?" Jessica said.

"Hardly anything that innocuous," Frank said dryly.

My face filled with heat and I stood up. "I had his permission. Like I said, I was looking for Mary. Anyway, now you have it. I'll talk to you later."

"We're not done here," Frank said.

"I have to get to Cecelia's. If you need more information, you know where to find me."

"Apparently not," Frank said. "Because it seems you're never actually where you say you're going to be."

I didn't answer. Instead, I stumbled out of the cafe, my hands reaching for the backs of the benches to help me along. It was hard to see through the tears of humiliation.

CHAPTER 16

I left the coffee shop with my humiliation quickly turning into fury. How dare he embarrass me in front of her? At this point, I didn't care if I ever talked to him again.

I took Old Bella to a "You Wash" car wash. She was grimier than usual and I needed help getting my mind off of Frank. And Jessica! That little smirk of hers! I smashed the sponge into the bucket.

I stood there with bubbles trickling down my arm and tried to get a grip on myself. *Focus on what's important. That poor dead boy and a murderer that is still walking free.* With grim determination to stay distracted, I cleaned the bus from top to bottom.

Then I drove to the Baker Street Bed and Breakfast. We were expecting guests that afternoon, and I was here to help flip the rooms. Cecelia was always observant, and somewhere between me organizing the already organized utensil drawer and moving the spices into an alphabetical order in the cupboard, she finally stopped me.

"So, young lady," Cecelia began. She always referred to me as a young lady when she was about to give me a serious talking to.

I paused, worried.

Her thin eyebrow lifted as she considered me. "You've been missing lately."

"Missing?" I asked. Was there something I'd forgotten to do?

"Yes, missing. You're not singing anymore."

"I... sing?"

"You certainly do. Oh, I hardly know what you're saying because you throw nonsense words in there. But still, you're always humming some song or another. And it's just been too quiet lately. And then there's this." She reached toward the counter and grabbed an unopened jar.

I recognized it right away. It was raspberry jam from last summer. I'd spent several hours in the hot sun, more than willing to pick them, despite the thorns, the bugs, the sunburn and the humidity. Cecelia's raspberry jam was to die for. Slathered on a slice of warm homemade bread, or a slice straight out of the toaster, it was better than any dessert you could get at the finest of restaurants.

"Yum," I said, still feeling confused as to why she was holding it out to me.

She shook the jar. "This is brand new."

"I see that," I said.

"I've had it on the counter for three days now, and you've not gotten into it. Usually, it's half gone by now. I've even caught you eating it straight with a spoon."

"Cecelia, to be fair, I was seven at the time."

"Seven, shmeven. I've seen you goop enough on the bread I wondered if you liked a wee bit of toast with your jam. Now, why haven't you gotten into it? Something's up. Out with it girl."

I groaned, not even knowing where to start. But I knew she wasn't going to give up so I might as well pour my heart out. "Last night, I found a piece of a cell phone from the scene of Jacob's first incident. And I learned that a gang tried to jump him at that very spot, only to be chased off by the owner of the land with a shotgun. Not only that, Jacob's family had been harassed before his death."

Cecelia quietly nodded as she grabbed a bottle of vinegar. She rumpled a newspaper and poured a splash of the liquid on to it, then began polishing a window. I waited, feeling breathless, for some sort of response to my tirade.

"Go on," was all she said. But it was all I needed to take off again.

"When I found Jacob, I took a bunch of photos. Unusable, I guess, but when I look at them now, I swear he'd been moved from the original scene. You already know how the police were only interested for a nano-second. Now they're satisfied no crime's been committed. Everyone's telling me that the kid fell down the stairs and to let it go. It's all very hush-hush." I shut the cupboard door and opened the next, staring at the cups like they were my enemy. "But it's not just me who's suspicious. Mary, the girl who asked for my help, wasn't convinced. And now she's disappeared, or at least I'm unable to find her. And the final straw is a big wad of money I found in the cave where she liked to hide. I think Jacob put it there. But anyone who knows anything has disappeared like rats down a sewer."

"My goodness! That is a lot! Everyone's disappeared?"

"Even his English roommate has apparently gone back into the Navy. And there's a girl he'd been with. I can't find her."

"A girl?"

"Yeah, he supposedly kissed some girl with a boyfriend and the boyfriend was going after Jacob. There was a time I wondered if that was why Jacob ended his Rumspringa."

"For a kiss?" Even chaste Cecelia didn't believe that story. "You don't know her name?"

"I agree. It *is* ridiculous, and so far, every road has been a dead end."

Cecelia started on another window, her eyebrows knitted together. "You might find this interesting. There's been a bit of gossip around the town about the banker's daughter. That girl is on the wrong track, for sure. They just got her back from Pittsburgh, and they've been trying to get her into rehab."

My hands froze.

"Really?" Perhaps Jacob had given the girl much more than a kiss, like drugs, giving her boyfriend a much bigger motive to come after him.

"Her father is playing it off like it isn't a big deal but he could barely crack a smile when I greeted him today. That poor man is under some serious stress."

I needed to find his daughter. "What was her name?"

"Amy Carmichael."

Of course. I knew her father, Scott Carmichael. He was a heavy-set man, going bald, but always with a smile on his face. He was more animated than one would expect from someone who ran the Sterling Bank but the customers loved him. He seemed like a real advocate for the people in this town, funding loans where other places had refused them.

"They live in that big house on the hill, right?" I asked. "He helped get you this place, didn't he?"

Cecelia nodded and her lips curved into a wide smile. "I'll see you at six."

"Six?" I asked pausing in my cup rearrangement.

"For dinner. Yes. I know you have some investigating to do. Now shoo." She chucked one of the balled-up newspapers at me. I laughed, feeling lighter than I had in a while. Maybe I had a real lead this time.

I headed out, but not before I grabbed a couple of cookies from the cookie jar.

Munching one—pecan snicker-doodle— I hopped into my van and cranked it over. That Carmichael house was right on the peak of White Horse Mountain. I just needed to go find it.

My search engine gave me the address with the same helpful 2.99 tip, and I plugged it into my GPS. I watched the pink ribbon route the way to the girl's house. There was just one problem.

What reason could I give her when I showed up?

CHAPTER 17

*I*t took nearly the whole drive there but I finally figured out an excuse to visit the banker. The answer was obvious and I blushed to think it had taken me so long. Mr. Carmichael had personally helped Cecelia buy the Baker Street Bed and Breakfast. There had been another woman who'd tried to block the sale and nearly was successful. But Mr. Carmichael had discovered that woman had secretly bid on the house herself and was able to squash any further roadblocks for Cecelia.

That's right. He'd really gone to bat for her. It had been three years now that the bed and breakfast had been in business, and obviously, I benefitted from my tour job with her, so it wasn't too out of the question for me to bring up a thank you card and maybe a bottle of wine, from both Cecelia and me.

Sort of a celebration gift that the business was staying in the green, which was something every banker would be happy about.

It meant that I had to return to town to get a card and a bottle of wine but I was happy to do it, and it wasn't long before I was on my way back up the mountain road.

The road curved sharply a few times, forcing me to slow down. I swallowed hard. The turns were just enough to bring back the memory of Derek. My hands tightened on the wheel as the scene played out before my eyes. His car crashing through the guardrail and rolling, end-over-end, to the bottom of the canyon.

A blasting horn made me jerk just in time to see a semi-truck heading straight for me. I yanked the steering wheel hard to get the van back into my own lane. What was I thinking? Stop!

My whole body trembled from the near miss. I turned into the nearest driveway and stopped the van. I covered my face with my hands, and a sob escaped me. I'd nearly killed someone because of my daydream. When, oh, when would these flashbacks stop?

I knew the answer. Not until I knew what really had happened that day. I couldn't accept the explanation that the fire chief had given me, that Derek committed suicide. He wouldn't do that to me, especially knowing I was in the car right behind him. He wouldn't.

I took a deep breath. *Now isn't the time. You're here to get information on Derek—No! Not Derek! Jacob!* With difficulty, I tried to pull my thoughts from the past and get a grip on the present.

Finally, when I felt like I'd regained some semblance of control, I continued down the road. It wasn't long before I found the Carmichael's driveway where I parked a few feet from the porch steps. Grabbing the wine and card, I climbed out and walked to the front door, trying to push away the memory of the truck horn that still blared in my ears. *Focus.* What kind of answers did I hope to find here?

I rang the doorbell and waited. A young woman, pretty and painfully thin, answered the door.

"Hello. My name's Georgie. I work for Cecelia Wagner. I was looking for your father. He helped us with some business stuff a while ago and I wanted to bring him this thank you gift." The words rushed out of my mouth as the young woman half-smiled.

"He's not here right now, but I can tell him you came by." She scratched at a sore on her cheek, making me wince.

I shifted a little, trying to think of how to start a conversation.

"Oh, I'm sorry I missed him. Do you think I could leave him a note?"

She looked pointedly at the card in my hand.

"Err, this is from my aunt. But I'd like to leave him a personal message of thanks myself if you don't mind."

She nodded, her fingers still scratching. "Yeah, sure. Why not. I think there's a pen in here." The girl left the door open and wandered down the hall.

I walked after her, glad to be inside. I'd write whatever I needed just to have a chance to talk with her.

The house was a bit ostentatious, with wealth painted in the high dollar lamps, rugs, and artwork. My mouth dropped to see an original Pablo Picasso. The family wasn't shy about the display of their money.

She led me into one room where an enormous executive desk sat in a corner. Facing forward was a picture of Mr. Carmichael. The heavy-set man was shaking hands with a former president. Humming a little, the girl rummaged through one of the drawers. "He actually gets a lot of thank you stuff like that from people around here."

Her comment made me feel a little foolish.

She pointed to a bar in the corner. "You can just set it there."

"That's nice that he's appreciated," I murmured. She wasn't kidding. On the bar were two potted plants already. And in the trash below was a plate of cookies still wrapped in plastic wrap.

I hurriedly looked away. "So, are you Amy?"

"That'd be me." Amy came over with a pen. I took it from her, at a loss again at how to start the conversation.

"Well?" She nodded to the envelope. "Aren't you going to write?"

"Oh, yeah. Sure." I pulled the envelope over and penned a generic; "Thank you for your help. We really appreciate it." Each scribbled word brought more panic as my time was running out.

Her phone dinged, and she lifted it to look at a notification.

My eyes flew open. The phone's screen was cracked, and I couldn't be certain, but it sure looked like a corner was missing.

"Wow, that looks like it's been through the wringer," I said airily, handing back the pen.

Amy didn't take her eyes from the screen. "Yeah," she said somewhat distracted. Her thumbs flew over the keyboard and then pressed send. "My new one is supposed to be here

148

tomorrow. Well, actually, yesterday. But you know how those things are."

"It can't be easy to use with the screen messed up like that. I know someone who can fix it. But then, if you're getting a new one, it doesn't matter."

"It's all good. Like I said, should be here tomorrow." She hid the phone against her belly. But this time I definitely saw it. The corner was missing.

My pulse thumped in my ears. She must have been at the scene. All the questions I'd thought I'd ask her dried up.

She stuck a piece of gum in her mouth and chucked the wrapper to lay next to the wine bottle. "You done?"

My mouth was too dry to answer so I nodded.

"C'mon then," she lazily waved to me and shuffled to the front door.

Do something! Say anything!

"Uh, I bet it gets lonely up on this hill." I rolled my eyes at my stupid comment.

"Nah, it's not too bad. Sometimes it's nice to be by myself."

"Yeah. Quiet is nice. Technology and the bustle of everything can be a lot." My point was stupid as she tapped her phone, but it was the best segue way I could think of for my next statement. "Like at the Amish village. You ever visit there?"

Amy's eyes narrowed. "Not really." She walked down the hall.

I followed with slow steps. "Yeah, except there was a terrible tragedy that happened there this week. To a young man named Jacob. You hear about it?"

"Nah, nothing," she said. Her voice had a bite and she opened the front door with force. "So you have a good day, hear?"

I threw out my trump card. "They aren't sure what happened to him but it sounds like the police are getting involved."

She made a startled noise and her hand froze on the doorknob.

My eyes locked onto hers. "Are you okay?" I tried to keep calm even though my own heart was racing.

"What do they think happened?"

I very gently shrugged. "They're suspecting foul play."

At those words, all the color left the woman's face, making the blemish pop out like a blood spot. "They think he was murdered?"

I shrugged again, unwilling to give up any more information.

"I might be able to track down more information. I'm friends with—"

She cut me off. "Thank you for coming but you need to go, now."

I nodded robotically and walked onto the front porch. Before the girl could completely close the door, I spun back.

"You know who did it. Was it your boyfriend?"

The door slammed shut.

I trudged back to the van, half-kicking myself for blurting that out, and half-renewed because I knew I was right. But what did that mean? Right, how?

CHAPTER 18

$\mathcal{B}$ack at home, I printed all the pictures I'd taken from the scene of Jacob's accident. My investment in the high-quality printer for the brochures for the tour company's portion of the bed and breakfast was coming into good use, and I felt rather proud when I saw the photos all laid out.

In reality, the pictures portrayed a bleak situation of Jacob's poor body, the boots, blood on the stairs, the piece of plastic, and all the little tidbits in between. It was only as I was looking through them again that I stopped at the boot.

I realized it didn't match what I'd seen the other Amish men wear. I knew the Amish all bought and wore the same style of shoe from the local department store. It was easy enough to pull the boots up on the internet and find images of their design.

Jacob's boot was black, like theirs, and would have continued to fool me except for the metal plate declaring the name. I searched the name brand and it took me to a high-end boot store website. Within minutes, I found the matching pair that sold for over two hundred dollars.

That was odd. Very odd. Why was he wearing boots like this? I flipped through the store's pictures, trying to puzzle it out. The sole on the bottom had a distinct jagged-knob pattern, with a circle around the letter K.

I froze, realizing I'd seen that imprint in the dirt all around the pond and Mary's cave hiding place. He *had* been there.

It didn't make sense that he'd keep his English boots if he was committing to the Amish lifestyle. But I didn't have the answer for that, so I set the observation aside.

Sighing, I searched up Amy Carmichael. There wasn't a lot on her, but there was a story about how the Carmichaels had moved to Gainesville about eight years ago. My eyebrow raised when I saw they all were from Pittsburgh, which is where I lived with Derek before his death. Pittsburgh was a big town, but it made me wonder what her dad had done there.

A few more searches brought up Amy's uncle, Mr.

Carmichael's brother. Now, this was interesting. It seemed he ran a laundry business, maybe in more ways than one.

So what was Jacob doing with Mr. Carmichael's daughter? Was it really just about some juvenile canoodling? Why did Jacob have all that money? And even weirder, what about his boots? Why hadn't he changed them out for more appropriate Amish wear?

I wondered about Amish hierarchy. Was there someone above an Elder? What if I went to their church and talked with their bishop? Could I convince him that something was going on? Maybe he could even help find Mary.

Thinking of the young girl decided it, and I grabbed my keys. I'd try it. What could I lose?

As USUAL, the community was bustling. I was surprised at how industrious the Amish were, knowing they'd been up hours before me, beginning work before the sun even peeked over the tree line. A few waved as I exited my car, seeming to become familiar with my presence in the community. I relaxed. They must not think I was all that bad. Maybe I was being paranoid about the orders not to talk to me.

I did wonder what they thought of my daily presence. Maybe

they just chalked it up to an English woman snooping around, attempting to educate herself with their simplistic life.

Taking in a cleansing breath, I walked up to the first group who was gathering the flowers from the front watering vases and carrying them inside.

"Hello, I'm Georgie."

"Yes, we know." A dark haired girl smiled and nodded. "Rebekah and Naomi have spoken of you."

I remembered that Naomi was Mary's friend. Odd that she mentioned me. "Yes, they are very kind. I was wondering where the...your bishop is?"

The young woman's smile faltered only a moment before she glanced at the church.

"Either in the church or at Sara and Jacob Goode's home. They have a new one to add to the flock, a beautiful baby boy."

It was strange to hear the terminology that was so normal to them.

"Oh, ok. Well, I'll check the church and if he isn't there I'll come back when he's less busy."

"I'll be happy to take you." The girl ducked her black-bonneted head and then turned and chattered to the others, her accent rolling out the Pennsylvanian Dutch language with beautiful fluidity. Then, back to me, "I'm Sara Moore."

"It's nice to meet you." I smiled and followed the girl down the street to the church.

Outside the building were several buggies with orange triangles on their backs. Horses whickered and swished their tails. We walked up the wooden steps and through the front doors. She led me down the center aisle to a room in the back.

Gently, she tapped the door.

"Ye can come in!" a voice called. Sara opened the door to reveal the bishop sitting at a desk with an enormous book before him.

"Bishop, this is Georgie Tanner. She'd care to speak with you, if ye have the time."

"Of course, come in." He waved me in. "Thank ye, Sara."

The girl nodded and left me alone with the Bishop, who motioned to the empty seat in front of his desk.

"Georgie Tanner. I've heard quite a bit about you lately." He was gray and grizzled but with a kind smile.

I nervously sat down, wondering exactly what he had heard. "I love your community and hope to educate our tourists who come visit. I appreciate the hospitality."

"Well, you're very welcome. What is it you would like me to help you with today?"

"Actually, sir..."

"Bishop is fine, dear."

I swallowed hard. "Bishop...there's another issue I was made aware of while I was here. Please let me explain everything and don't blame those who wanted to help."

His lips pressed together and I felt my pulse quicken as I pulled out the photographs. I selected only the ones with the boot and internet search results of the boots and the cell phone piece. I reached across the desk, handing him the photos. His eyes didn't leave mine as he took them.

"I had assumed there was a secondary reason for your visit. We're not fond of lying, here."

"I wasn't lying, sir, I really do want to know more about the community. But then I learned about Jacob. I have had...some experience, I guess you can say, with looking into odd cases around our area."

"A parishioner has already admitted his guilt over the death of young Jacob. I don'a see why we need anything else said or done about this." His jaw tightened.

I flinched at the words but pressed forward. "With all due respect, I believe someone murdered that young man.

157

Someone with wealth and power and who had a reason to want him gone. I think he was moved to the bottom of those stairs and someone is still out in the town and walking around, free and able to do such things again."

His face drew closed like a wall had come down. It was as if I hadn't even spoken. "When did you get so close to his body to sully it this way?"

"I'm sorry?" I was confused. "I didn't sully it. He was actually alive and I was waiting for help. But something felt wrong so I took the pictures to study when I had more time."

The man gathered the pictures and handed them back to me. "I do not appreciate you taking advantage of our more naive and innocent people, tricking them into letting you play policewoman. I do not appreciate you desecrating his body, nor taking these images of him. I want you gone. Do not come on this property again."

"Sir, I..." I was shocked.

"Get out!"

His command made me jump. I grabbed the pictures, feeling tears well in my eyes, and ran through the church back to my van.

CHAPTER 19

I drove aimlessly for a while, slipping back into my old habit to cope with stress. When I finally realized where I was, I was hours from home, tired and hungry.

But I didn't want to go home and face that quiet apartment. And I didn't want to go to Cecelia's, as much as I loved her. I just couldn't deal with the chance of running into Frank right now.

So moonlight saw me standing on the porch of the only other place I knew to go. I hesitated and then knocked.

"I'm coming. Hold your horses," yelled the grouchy old man I'd become so very fond of.

He opened the door and blinked at me, his eyes enormous

behind his coke-bottle reading glasses. "You?" he asked, mouth dropping like I was a two-headed goat that had just escaped from the circus.

I shifted my weight to the other foot. "Yeah. Me. Can I come in?"

He took a step back, his mouth still hanging open. It was then that Peanut realized there were visitors and came racing down the hallway from the living room as if her very steps were powered by barking.

"Confound it. Georgie's already inside. You're useless as a guard dog," Oscar said, waving his hand at the pup. He shut the door. "You were just snoring with your feet chasing after sleep bunnies, you little faker."

Peanut quieted as soon as she saw it was me and now jumped to get my attention, her front claws repeatedly raking down my shin.

"Ow. Ow. Ow. Come here." I scooped her up to save my skin. Then I stood holding her, watching for Oscar's reaction. I buried half my face in the top of her furry head.

He slipped off his glasses and studied me. He must have seen something he took pity on because he nodded. "Come now. Let's get some tea."

He retied his bathrobe as he shuffled into the kitchen, his

slippers scuffing against the worn vinyl. Once inside, I could tell Oscar had been busy. The kitchen looked a might better than normal, with the usual leaning tower of dishes missing from the sink.

After a minute of grunting and grumbling, he located his tea kettle and filled it up. He set it on the stove and turned the burner on, then set about to retrieving two mugs.

"Carol always said chamomile was what you drank at night." He sighed and rifled through the box. "But you're getting this fancy Rose stuff because I can't find nothing else."

I smiled. "That'll be great."

"You want some toast?"

"All right," I said.

"Good, because that's all you're getting. I'm not a short-order cook." He undid the twist on the bread bag and soon had two slices popped into a very old toaster. The glow from the overhead light was softer than normal since one of the bulbs had burned out. Soon he was scraping butter on the toast, the kettle was whistling, the dog panting at my feet. And I was doing nothing.

I was at the end of myself.

He brought over the toast and then came back with the mugs, clanking together slightly in his arthritic hand.

"You dunk the bags," he instructed me and I stifled another smile.

"Got it," I said, opening the paper wrapper and following his example like I'd never done it before. We did that for a few moments, exaggerated dunks of the tea bag before he pronounced it was done.

"Come here, Bear," he called the dog.

The Pomeranian was happy at my feet. Oscar grabbed a piece of the toast and whistled between his teeth. The little fluff ball sprang away to his side.

"Like a lady," he said gently, and the dog daintily took the tidbit. He scooped her up and plopped her on his lap, where he proceeded to pet her rather aggressively. But her happy eyes showed she didn't mind one bit.

"Now, what's got you out this late and at my door? You got trouble with the police?"

I cracked a smile then. I couldn't help myself. "No. Just feeling kind of —" I sighed.

"Oh. Mmm." He nodded a bit and took a sip of his tea. "The dolty-waggers. I get it."

"The... what?"

He waved at me impatiently. "You know, that feeling that

wants to bring you down, but you can't let it. So you have to pretend you're fighting it even if it seems like you're losing."

I nodded. He got it.

"What brought them about this time?" he asked.

I cupped my mug, relishing the heat. Slowly, I told him the whole story, from meeting Mary, to finding Jacob, to the police, the cave, and finally the visit with the bishop.

Listening, he ate his toast and brushed the crumbs off the table, most of them landing on top of Peanut. Occasionally he grunted or nodded in acknowledgment of some detail or another. At the end of my story, I sat there feeling like a deflated balloon.

"You know, when an animal comes across something they don't like, they naturally shy away," he said, his eyebrows lifting sagely.

What in the world? After everything I said, that was his response? "Uh, okay," I answered, more than a little disappointed.

"They just do it. Only human beings try to argue themselves out of their gut feeling. One of the hardest lessons to learn in this life is to trust your gut." He took a sip of tea.

"So, you're saying..."

"Confound it." He scowled. "What is it with today's generation? Electronics scramble everyone's brain? If you think something's wrong, then chances are something's wrong. Instead of trying to think of ways to win people over to your way of thinking, focus instead on who did it and their motives. Put yourself in the killer's shoes. You can't convince people to believe anything but what they want. But you can focus on digging out the truth for yourself."

Peanut chose that moment to sit up and scratch her ear. Crumbs showered everywhere. Oscar set her on the floor, muttering, "What are you trying to do? Castrate me?"

The dog smiled up at him, black eyes sparkling and tongue hanging out. "Go on," he shooed. "Get to your bed."

Peanut scampered off. A moment later, I heard springs squeaking. He glowered. "In my bed, apparently." He looked at me, guiltily. "Don't be thinking that's usual. She only gets to do that on special occasions."

She did it too naturally for me to believe that but I let him off the hook by nodding.

He cleared his throat. "Anyway, back to your situation. Who are your suspects?"

It was so refreshing to have someone believe me and to want to know what I was thinking, that several names tumbled out of my mouth. It took me off guard that I must have, subconsciously, suspected them all along.

"There's Amy and her boyfriend. And then there was a note left by Mary in her cave, saying the fat man was coming. I've met three so far, Elder Yoder, Mr. Murray, and Mr. Carmichael. Maybe one of them is involved." I chewed my thumbnail. "Everything about Elder Yoder told me he did not like Jacob. It may even be his fault that Jacob died, through neglected medical care. Jacob caused Mr. Murray a lot of problems, not the least being he drove the man's tractor into the pond. There was a rumor going around that Jacob kissed Amy, Mr. Carmichael's daughter. It's one reason I really suspect her boyfriend. Plus the gang that attacked Jacob is more in their age range."

"You got some solid suspects. That's good. But don't cross everyone else around him out. Even the closest to him, a friend, a sister, a mom, could have a motive."

I thought about it. "Oh, I doubt it."

He guffawed. "Sure. Like that girl Mary? Interesting she's missing now."

"Interesting...how?"

"She had a crush on him, right? Maybe realized he wasn't ever going to return those affections. Heard he kissed another girl... wouldn't be the first murder to happen that way. Didn't you say she found him?"

"But she's disappeared!"

"Right. Happens all the time."

My mouth dropped open. "You're saying she's run away."

He closed his eyes and shook his head. "Confound electronics. Of course, that's what I'm saying."

I sat back in the chair, considering. Honestly, my mind was blown. "I was looking in a completely different direction. Amy Carmichael's uncle owns a laundry business out in Columbus. I was a little suspicious of that."

"Hmm? What's that?" Now it was his turn to look surprised. "Mikey's Laundry. You telling me she's related?"

"Yeah," I nodded, curious. "What do you know?"

"I don't know nothing about no Amy Carmichael. But Mikey's Laundry was on our radar a long time ago. Back when I was with the Feds. Them and their sister company, Midnight Trucking."

My world reeled at his pronouncement. I clutched my chest and reminded myself to breathe. It's just a coincidence.

It had to be.

CHAPTER 20

"What?" I managed to whisper.

"What, what??" Oscar asked back, his eyebrows wrinkling crossly.

I gripped my mug tightly. "Can you tell me more about the trucking company?"

He put his glasses back on and peered at me through them. Sighing, he slid them off. "You're as white as a ghost. Midnight Trucking. Did runs between Pittsburgh, Cleveland, Columbus, and over to Detroit. One operation I was overseeing during my time in the FBI was to watch them. Actually caught their trucks on a boat headed over Lake Erie to Canada once or twice. Every time we started to close in, they slipped out of our hands. We had a snitch somewhere in the line."

"What were they hauling?"

He shrugged, his thumb rubbing the red knuckles on his other hand. "Who knows for sure. Rumor has it that it was money. Guns. Drugs. All the basics for bad guys."

"But not everyone who works there knew it. Right? Because some of their business was legitimate. Right?" Desperation for him to say yes made me nearly choke.

"What is going on with you? Yeah. Yeah. Sure. Whatever makes you feel better."

I stood up, holding on to the back of the chair for balance. My pulse whooshed in my ears. "I've got to go."

"You sure are strange tonight."

"I'm sorry. I'll see you tomorrow, okay?" I grabbed my jacket and headed to the door.

"Fine. But next time don't forget my turnover!"

I didn't respond, instead slammed the door and pounded down the stairs. My hands were shaking so badly I almost dropped the key as I climbed into the van.

Only one thing was in my mind, rolling over and over, driving every thought out.

Derek's new job had been at Midnight Trucking.

I remembered a while back Oscar seemed startled when I'd mentioned Derek's last name was Summers. I wondered if he'd forgotten about that conversation, or if he was playing me to see what I knew.

I was almost home when I got a text from Frank. —**Hey! Where've ya been?**

I didn't answer, instead clicking my phone off. I needed to be alone. Once upstairs, I went straight to the bathroom. I opened the medicine cabinet and pushed everything to one side until I found what I was looking for.

My sleeping pills. I needed them tonight.

I woke up the next morning feeling groggy like my head was stuffed with wet cotton. It took a second for the memories of last night to filter back in, and when they did, I pressed my eyes tight. Hot tears trickled down my face and I twisted the sheet in frustration. After a few sniffles, I got up and got some coffee, and sat with a thump at the table. The easel had been bumped at some point last night and the painting now faced the sunlight.

Flowers. Green.

Angrily, I grabbed my biggest paintbrush and squeezed out black paint onto my palette. I crushed it until the entire tube was empty and then I slashed the paint onto the canvas. Lies! All lies! I didn't realize I was crying until a sharp sob forced itself out of my throat. All those years! I thought Derek was an art consultant. I actually thought he helped people. But really he worked for smugglers? Lies!

When the canvas was as black as my heart felt, I stopped. The paintbrush slipped from my fingers and fell to the floor. The emotion was gone. I felt numb.

There was nothing I could do about Derek. I had to pack all that away and not think about it. At least not right now.

But I could still help Jacob.

I drained my coffee and swiped my hair into a ponytail. And then I was out the door and running to my van.

There were other things Oscar had told me last night that I needed to follow. And the most important to me right now was to trust my gut.

My gut told me that, somehow, Amy was in the middle of this. She had the jealous boyfriend. She had the broken phone case. She reacted weirdly when I talked to her yesterday.

I knew she was getting a new cell phone today. Maybe I could do a little reconnaissance.

I took the switch-backs up the mountain road recklessly. There was no place to hide near the Carmichael's house, so I parked in an empty driveway next door and hoped the owners wouldn't be back any time soon. Then I pushed through the neighbor's trees to settle behind a bush where I had a good view of the Carmichael's house.

Part of me couldn't believe I was doing something so brash and ridiculous. But another part, the part still stunned by last night's news, didn't care.

The driveway was empty, but it had been that way when I came yesterday so I had no reason to think Amy wasn't there. I sat for a long while, waiting for who knew what. Finally, I turned on my phone to distract myself. Red notifications flashed in my messages, and I saw I had a few from both Frank and Cecelia.

Deciding that I'd better deal with them, I opened Cecelia's first.

—GiGi, can you come for morning set up?

—GiGi, the guests are here. Are you coming?

—GiGi! Where are you? This isn't like you at all. Are you okay?

Guilt flooded me and I quickly typed back. —**I'm so sorry. Horrible day today, and my phone was off. Can I come in later?**

While I waited for her response, I opened Frank's. —**Want to get together with me and Jessica later?**

His second said,—**Hey? Are you ignoring me?**

And then, —**Where are you?**

There was nothing I wanted to say. I sent Frank back, — **Nothing wrong. Talk with you later.**

Cecelia responded then with a—**Sweetie, you scared the tar out of me. Glad to know you're okay. You just rest and feel better.**

I smiled. I sure loved that woman.

I scrolled a moment to find my notepad and brought it up. Settling back into the nest of pine needles under the tree, with my back against the trunk, I cast a glance at the house to be sure I still couldn't be seen.

All was quiet and clear on that front.

I started to type my list of suspects that I'd given Oscar the night before. Under that, I listed my clues.

*money roll with drug bag

*broken piece of a cell phone case

*same boot prints of all sizes at pond

*Jacob wearing English boots, not Amish

*tractor going into pond despite him being good with mechanics

*Mary's note about the man coming to the cave

*Mary's note saying she didn't want to hide Jacob's secret

*Amy being brought home to be put into rehab

*Mary has a crush on Jacob

I studied the list, chewing the inside of my cheek. I knew the answer was there but it was still blocked from me. Something about a drug ring? But who killed Jacob? And how did he end up at the bottom of the Amish wheelhouse stairs?

These questions were going to be the death of me. I shut the list and opened up my drawing app. It was a cool thing that allowed different colors, textures, and paintbrushes.

I chose the painting brush and cadmium red. I needed vibrant, something to match how my emotions felt at the moment. With my fingertip, almost carelessly, I swirled the brush across the horizon.

Red at night... sailor's delight.

The red captured my eyes like a spurt of blood in untouched snow. What was it about red that was drawing my attention? I frowned as I stared at the painting.

On a whim, I chose straw-brown to be the next color and dragged my finger in a zig-zag down the side. I added another and connected them with lines.

A set of stairs. Just like the ones that led to the wheelhouse.

I stiffened. Wait a minute. What was it that Mary had said about Elder Yoder? That above all cost, he had to protect the Amish name from being sullied? That was it!

A sound grabbed my attention, the grinding of tires on the gravel driveway. I couldn't think about it anymore and powered my phone off to watch.

CHAPTER 21

The car coming down wasn't the one I expected—a UPS or some other delivery service. Instead, it was a blue sedan with a spoiler.

I ducked my head as the car rumbled by and then leaned around the trunk to see who got out.

The door opened and a young man, I guessed close to Amy's age, emerged. This must be the boyfriend. He glanced around, making my heart skip a beat, but then walked up to the front door.

It opened before he had a chance to knock, and Amy sprang out onto the porch. There was a long embrace and then she led him inside, shutting the door behind them.

I crept forward slowly, looking for an open window.

Carefully, I made it to the edge of the trees and then scurried, hunched over, for the back of the car. My heart beat hard as I peered around the bumper.

Nothing came from inside the house.

Still bent over, I raced to the corner of the porch. I clutched the railing and tried to catch my breath which was raised from the adrenaline ripping through my veins.

Everything was still and quiet. An owl hooted in the distance, and vehicle noise came from the road.

I crept along the side of the house and crouched under the window. Voices could be heard now, and it sounded like arguing. I started to go farther down the side of the house when a storage shed at the back of the property caught my attention.

Was I hearing noises from there, too?

Apprehensively, I hurried down the path to the large wooden shed, the skin on my neck prickling. The doors were shut with a padlock. I walked around the small building but there were no windows. On my way back to the front, I accidentally snapped a stick in half. I froze.

"Is someone out there? Please!" A voice called. I recognized it right away. Mary.

I wanted to reassure her but I didn't want her to do something that would cause the two in the house to get suspicious. Instead of responding, I hid behind the corner of the shed and prayed they hadn't heard her. My muscles jerked as the door from the house slammed. I juggled my cell phone from my pocket and turned it on.

The screen was frozen.

"Now what are you planning to do?" Amy yelled. I heard footfalls then, and they were coming closer. A second set sounded like a person running to catch up.

"You did this to me," the man growled.

"Shut up. You know this wasn't me," Amy whined back. "Now be nice to her."

"You had your chance to get her to talk about where the money was. Now it's my turn."

I stared at my phone in desperation. The little wheel spun as it tried to boot up. *Come on. Come on!*

There was a scrape of the key against the lock and then the shed shook as the door was flung open.

"Get over here, you maggot," the man yelled.

"Please. I won't tell. Just let me go home," Mary begged.

I looked around for anything on the ground that I could use as a weapon. Some small rocks, tiny branches, that was it.

CEECE JAMES

Then I heard a metallic click. My mouth went dry.

"You know what this is?" said the guy. "This is my friend, switchblade. We ain't going to play any games anymore. You tell me where that money is, or I'll take your fingers, one by one. Maybe send them home to your momma, hmm?"

"No!" Mary screamed.

"Oh, for crying out, loud. Stop it, Tom," Amy muttered. "Seriously. You're creeping me out."

"You think your mom would like a finger? Which one? This one?" Tom said.

Mary screamed again.

"The money. Where is it?" he asked, his voice sounding low and calm.

"It's—it's in the cave. By the pond," Mary sobbed.

"There now. That wasn't so hard, was it? And you get to keep all your fingers." There was scuffling and the sounds of dragging. I peeked around the corner to see Tom haul Mary out with her arm twisted behind her back. Mary's dress was torn and her face was dirty. "Now, you're coming with us to make sure we find it."

Amy rolled her eyes. "Us? Seriously? You need me, too?"

178

"Who's going to hold the gun on her while I drive? Now, get in the car."

"You have a gun, too? Kind of over-kill, don't you think?" Amy grumbled.

"Just get in the car." He kicked the shed door shut with his boot. I noticed it was the same brand as the one Jacob had worn.

I watched, helpless, as Amy trudged back to the house where the car waited. Tom followed, dragging a whimpering Mary with him.

I glanced at the edge of the property and then back at the trio before making a dash for the trees. As quietly as I could, I pushed my way through the branches and underbrush to the neighbor's yard. I ran up the driveway to my van and climbed in, too afraid to shut the door. I was sure that the sound would carry over to the Carmichael's house.

But leaving the door open had its advantage because I was able to hear the sedan start and drive out to the road, sounding like the tires spun out on the gravel before catching the pavement.

As the sedan noise faded, I slammed my door and started Old Bella. She whirred over and over, failing to catch.

"Come on," I begged, pumping the gas. The final pump did it

and she started with a misfire and plume of black smoke. I backed her up and got out onto the road.

There was no one around. I was the only one on the road.

"Where are you?" I whispered, leaning over the wheel. Did they go up the mountain instead of down? That didn't make sense. My engine roared as I pushed Old Bella to her limit; racing on the straight strips, and braking on the curves. I didn't want to lose Mary.

I nearly cried when I caught sight of the sun hitting the chrome of the blue sedan. It was just up ahead. The car disappeared around a curve. I stomped on the gas and followed.

The road was precarious. A steep drop-off cradled one side with a bank on the other. My tires chirped as I hit another corner, trying to keep up.

As I came back around the bend, I saw a pale face looking back out the rear window at me. It was Amy. And then Mary did as well. Amy yelled something to Tom who stomped on the gas even harder.

My stomach sank as the car whipped around the next corner. The van swayed as I tried to keep them in sight.

I had to quickly think of a plan. What did I hope to do? I couldn't stop them up here on this road. It was dangerous.

And to make it worse, there was a sharp corner ahead; dead man's curve.

Thinking of Mary, I eased off the gas, hoping that by backing off, Tom would drive safer.

The curve was less than a quarter mile ahead. They weren't slowing down. If anything, they were still accelerating even as the space between our vehicles grew.

The sedan swerved as it entered the next curve, kicking up dust. Somehow, Tom regained control and brought it back on the road. I could see Amy hitting him on the shoulder. He yelled back and twisted the wheel to take the next corner just as sharp. The car hugged the center line.

There were just three more turns. And then two. I wanted to close my eyes. *Please slow down. Please. Please.*

Tom revved up to take the last turn. Mary moved to look back at me. Her eyes were sad and she held up her hand to say goodbye.

I was once again, helpless to do anything.

CHAPTER 22

I heard the sedan's tires screech from inside the van. And then metal against metal. Broken glass. I hit my brakes and slowed to a crawl. I didn't want to see what I knew was ahead. I couldn't bear to be a spectator to another car fire.

Get moving! My inner voice screamed. *You don't have the luxury of feeling sorry for yourself right now. See if you can help.*

I bit my lip to the point I tasted blood and stepped on the gas to take the turn. The first thing that met me was a cloud of dust. The next, a guardrail that had been bent like a banana peel. I stopped at the end of the corner and threw on my flashers before jumping out of the van.

By some miracle, the car had only dropped ten feet, caught by a grove of trees. It lay on its side, the rear tire still spinning. Smoke plumed from the radiator. My breathing was ragged as I tried to calm myself down. There were no sounds coming from the disabled vehicle.

I skirted around the guardrail and slid down the embankment. It was smoky in the car but I tried to peer inside.

The shattered windshield busted the rest of the way open through some ferocious kicks, and a very angry Tom climbed out, shouting words my grandma would have slapped me for. He half-fell off the hood and crawled over to the side of the car. He stood, trying to catch his breath with one hand on his knees.

Unbelievably, he had a gun in the other. He turned and saw me and his eyes narrowed. He lifted the pistol in my direction, though it bobbed and weaved with his unsteadiness.

I held my hands up. "Let's not do anything crazy. You might really be hurt. Let me get you some help."

The passenger door banged open and Amy popped out. The door hit the top of Tom's head, making him scream again. Amy climbed out while Tom crouched to the ground. He held his head as blood poured out, seemingly oblivious of the gun in his hand.

Watching my footing, I hurried over and wrenched the gun away. Carefully, I edged a few feet back.

"You stupid idiot!" Amy screamed, her thin arms railing in the air. "I told you to slow down! Now, look what you did!" She slapped him on his back and then tried to scramble up the hill.

"Stop right there!" I yelled.

She turned and her eyes tried to focus on me. "You talking to me?"

"Yes. Stay right there."

"I don't know what you're thinking, but we just got into a car accident. Flipped over the deadman's curve. I think I'll stand where I like," she said defiantly.

"You stay there or I'll shoot." I clicked back the hammer.

Her mouth dropped open. She raised one hand while the other went for the sore on her cheek.

"Mary?" I yelled. "Mary? You okay?"

The young girl climbed out of the same passenger door and darted around Tom to my side.

"Okay," I said to Amy. "You just sit next to your boyfriend and chill out. I'm going to call for help."

She rolled her eyes but did what I asked.

I didn't trust her. I pulled my cell phone from my pocket, not taking my eyes off the couple.

"Mary, I need you to help me here, okay?" I said.

"I don't know how." Her voice was shaky.

"I know. You've had a hard time. But you can do this. Just take my phone. Push the bump on the bottom. That's a button. Now touch the glass and slide your finger up." I couldn't risk taking my eyes off of the two standing in front of me. "At the bottom is a green picture. I need you to touch it. Now look for the name, Frank. Press it, please."

"I—I did it," Mary said shakily.

"Great. Hold it to your ear. Let me know if you hear anything."

She held it up, jerking slightly at the ringtone. Her wide eyes caught mine.

"It's okay. Just let me know if someone answers."

I could hear Frank yell, "Georgie! Are you okay?"

Mary squealed at the sound of his voice.

"It's okay," I told her. "Tell him to come up White Horse Mountain road. Tell him to bring the cavalry because I have a gun on two suspects."

"You won't shoot," Tom said with a sneer.

"Don't bet on it," I said. "I've done it before." I hadn't really, but he didn't know that.

Mary's voice wavered as she relayed my message.

Frank's voice thundered through the receiver. "Let me talk to her."

"Mary," I said calmly. "Hold the phone away from you. You see those little circles that come up?"

She nodded.

"Push the third one from the left on the top row."

Her finger quavered as she reached for it, and then Frank's voice ripped through the air.

"Frank," I said. "You're on speaker. I have the bad guys. Can you get your helpful black-and-white car up here? Like pronto? Because one is daring me to shoot him, and since I found him hurting Mary, I'm sorely tempted."

Tom turned green at my words.

"On my way," Frank growled.

Mary held the phone with uncertainty. Her gaze jumped between me and the two people sitting on the ground.

"Why don't you head up to the road," I said. "Stand behind the guardrail and watch for the police. You see anything, holler at me."

She did as I asked, and it wasn't long before we could hear the distant yowling of sirens echoing off of the mountain.

Frank, Jefferson, and a whole pile of officers carefully came down the hill. They handcuffed Tom and Amy and led them up the bank. A tow truck was called to deal with the car.

"Why would you kill that Amish boy?" Frank asked Amy as he led her to his car.

"I didn't kill anyone!" She lunged against the handcuffs.

"Sit down," Jefferson said. He pushed her into the back of his car. "Let me read you your rights."

Tom got the same treatment in the other car. He scowled at me through the window. I gave him my best smile and pageant wave.

Frank came over and started to give me a hug. But he must have known something was still off between us because he stopped just short and took a step back. His gaze fell to the ground and the toothpick moved to the other side of his mouth.

"I'm sorry about the hard time I gave you. I didn't believe you, but you did it anyway," he finally said. "You captured Jacob's killer."

I lifted my chin. "Not yet, I haven't."

CHAPTER 23

"What?" Frank asked, clearly confused. He narrowed his eyes and removed the toothpick from his mouth. Using it, he pointed to the police cars. "Who do we have back there, then?"

"Them?" I said. "You have the guys that threatened Jacob, and I dare-say if you get Kari's HOA to come, they'd identify them as part of the group of drug dealers who've been working their neighborhood. You've also got two people who kidnapped an Amish girl, trying to get their drug money back. That's who you've got there."

"But not Jacob's murderer." He raised an eyebrow.

I shook my head. "No."

He nodded and put the toothpick back in his mouth. "You

plan on telling me who did it, or am I going to find out through another phone call?"

"I didn't plan on—"

"Yeah, yeah. I know. You didn't plan on this happening. But it did." He spit this time.

My heart filled with sorrow when I looked at him. He didn't realize what I'd been through since learning about Derek. He didn't realize the wall that went up, and how I didn't know if I could ever let it down again. A part of me just didn't know how to care anymore.

"I guess that's true," I admitted with a sigh.

"What's going on with you?" he asked.

I wasn't going to get into it now. Not with the cavalry all around me with their lights and gruff commands and an Amish girl shivering under a wool blanket two feet away.

"Later," I said. "Now do you want to know who killed Jacob or not?"

"Yeah. I do."

"It was Mr. Carmichael," I said.

"I can't wait to hear this. How do you figure?" Frank asked.

I nodded to Mary. "She's going to be key to all of this. Jacob hid his drug money in her hiding place and made her keep it a secret. Mr. Carmichael brought his daughter here to get her clean by admitting her into treatment. He saw her getting into trouble, knew she was running with Jacob and his roommate, Dylan. He did something to Dylan that scared him back into the military—if that's really where he is. He also went after Jacob to try to do the same thing. Maybe it was an accident, and Mr. Carmichael went too far. He was desperate to save his daughter."

"How did Jacob end up in the wheelhouse?"

"Elder Yoder. I'm guessing Mary went to him for help when she found Jacob. What she didn't realize was that Elder Yoder would pose him at the bottom of the stairs like that."

"Okay. Why do you think he did that?"

"The Elder had said that he wouldn't let anything sully the Amish name. And what Jacob did was sully it. To be a drug dealer, murdered by an angry father. So Elder Yoder moved him to the Amish property and then let it be known that Jacob was drunk and had fallen down the stairs. Imbibing in too much alcohol, well, that's shameful, but only on his family, and not on the community at large. He also put Jacob's English boots back on his feet to show the community how Jacob never truly committed to the Amish ways. It was a secret language they understood."

"And the blood on the stairs?"

"Came from a cut on his own hand. I noticed Elder Yoder kept his hand in his pocket when I first met him, and then later, I saw a bandage on it. The whole thing was a scene set up for the Amish. But Mary knew what really happened, and she hoped to get help for her friend before he died." I looked at the girl who trembled in her blanket. "But Jacob was too far gone. Mr. Carmichael had used a weapon, probably one of the old pipes I saw lying in a pile by the pond, and cracked him on the skull."

Frank's jaw muscles jumped as he clenched it. He glanced at Mary and then at Jefferson.

"But you'll have to find the proof. I can't do everything for you." I said that last bit jokingly. Old habits die hard.

With that, I climbed into my van. I knew there would be lots of questions later and probably a long visit to the station.

Frank opened the passenger side. "You mind taking this little lady home?" he asked, his hand on Mary's shoulder.

I smiled at her. "Absolutely not. It would be my pleasure."

"And then dinner later, maybe?"

My gaze flicked up to his and I shrugged and then shook my head no. "I'm just tired, Frank. I think I want to be alone."

He locked eyes with me then. The intensity made me blush. "You know I love you, right?" he gruffly whispered.

My mouth opened, and I couldn't answer. There was no time anyway because he disappeared from the doorway and Mary hopped in. I was still staring out the passenger door when it closed, ending with his usual, Tap! Tap! on the side to let me know it was all clear.

"Miss Tanner?" Mary whispered.

I glanced at her. "Uh, yes, let's get you home, shall we?"

She nodded and pulled the blanket tighter around her.

"Seatbelts!" I said.

Mary looked at me blankly. I shook my head at how silly I was and buckled it around her. Then slowly, I pulled on to the road.

The sun had set by now, and dusk folded in like gray curtains. It took a few minutes of small talk, but I eventually got Mary to open up. It turned out that she'd made one last trek to the cave. Tom had seen her and grabbed her. He'd been upset about the money that Jacob had taken, and he knew how the two of them had been friends. He'd seen her there the week before when the gang had tried to get the money back the first time.

"So what happened that day?" I asked Mary.

"So Jacob saw the car pull up and the boys jump out. He told me that was his gang, and then told me to hide, so I ran into the blueberry bushes. He tried to talk to them, but they weren't going to listen, going on and on about the money. I just would have given it to them, I swear, but I didn't want to disobey Jacob. When they started closing in on him, Jacob got on the tractor. I saw him pushing and pulling various things, and then he started it up and drove into the pond, honking the horn the whole time. Mr. Murray showed up with his gun and they all scattered."

The boot tracks of different sizes but with all the same tread finally made sense. The gang must have worn the same boots as their sign. "Why did he drive the tractor into the pond?"

"I think he thought if he was in the center of the water, they couldn't get at him. Or maybe Mr. Murray would see it going in the water and come running faster. I don't know for sure."

I nodded. "After Tom grabbed you, what happened?"

"They locked me up in that little room. Told me to keep quiet or they'd hurt my mom." Her lip trembled and she stared at her hands. "Brought me food and drinks in a can."

"They didn't hurt you?" I asked, carefully.

She shook her head and I breathed a sigh of relief.

"So are you hungry now?" I asked.

She wrinkled her nose. "I'm not too fond of English food," she admitted, making me laugh.

"What did you eat?"

"Food in these funny little trays. Everything came in bags."

I nodded. That sounded about right, and I could imagine how weird for someone who'd only eaten everything made from scratch.

"There's just one thing I don't understand," I murmured more to myself.

"What?"

"How did Amy's cell phone get broken?"

"Oh, she was there."

That made me sit up. "She was? When?"

"When that fat man hit Jacob."

My mouth dropped. "You saw it?"

She nodded, solemnly. "Yes. The girl showed up first. I was watching from my cave. Jacob talked to her and gave her something. Then the fat English man showed up. The girl tried to stop him and the man shoved her down. He had a metal pipe in his hands and he hit Jacob. The man told Jacob never to talk to his daughter again and then yanked her away. That's when I got Elder Yoder."

I nodded. Amy's phone must have broken when she landed on the ground from being shoved.

"Is that when you wrote the note in your mom's poem book?"

She looked scared. "You saw that? Oh, momma will be so displeased."

I patted her on the knee. "I have a feeling she's going to be too happy to see you to care. Don't worry."

OF COURSE, I was right. When Rebekah saw her daughter, she fell to the floor in tears. I almost lost it myself watching the mom and daughter hug. Then Rebekah insisted I stay for tea, and sent her oldest daughter out at a full run. A few minutes later, the daughter returned with the bishop.

His face was stern as Mary and I recounted the story. I was afraid for the young girl, but he said that the ordeal she'd been through was enough to teach how important openness and honesty was to the community.

I wasn't sure how much of that honesty would be conveyed to Elder Yoder but that wasn't my battle.

The bishop ended with, "If we can bring anything good out of this, other than the discovery of the person who harmed Jacob, it is that we have been given the gift of life in having our sweet Mary returned to us." The bishop turned back to me. "Ye are welcome in our community and we are more than happy to help ye learn more about our culture. I do ask, though, that ye don't use modern devices or call in the authorities, without prior discussion with me and the others."

Of course, I agreed right away, very pleased to have my permission to visit Sunny Acres reinstated. It was a happy ending as far as I was concerned.

CHAPTER 24

*I*t was five o'clock and Frank was sitting on my couch. I know I'd said I wanted to be alone, but his last comment to me proved I owed it to him to at least tell him about my conversation with Oscar.

I didn't know what it all meant with Derek working for the trucking company. But it brought up the fact that I might not have known my fiancé as well as I'd believed. To love someone and find out they were still a stranger, that thought shook me to my core.

I'd bleakly told Frank as I paced the living room, each step driven by anxiety and shame for what I'd missed.

Frank's response was sweet. "Come, sit." He patted the cushion next to him and then he held me when I finally collapsed next to him in tears. He murmured words I didn't understand, but his arms and soft kisses said all I need to hear.

Finally, I calmed down. I looked up into his face and gave him a grateful smile.

"Georgie. I've got you. We'll figure this out." He brushed my hair from my face. "One step at a time. But let's not think the worst about Derek yet. Let's get all the facts first and not just jump straight in."

"Isn't that enough facts?" I hated crying. It felt like my whole head was swelling. I could only imagine how I looked.

"This is why you couldn't be a cop. You can't just look at the face value. There's a lot more to it."

"But what about my gut feeling?" I asked, remembering Oscar.

"Gut feelings do come into play. But those feelings can be tricky, especially when love is on the line." He cupped my face in one of his hands, his thumb softly stroking my cheek. "You owe it to him to give him the benefit of the doubt until we learn more."

I fell back into Frank's arms and allowed him to draw me in. Allowed him to let me feel safe, to be vulnerable once more.

"Thank you, Frank."

"For what? This is as natural as breathing to me."

"Comforting me?" I asked.

"No. Loving you."

I smiled. "You really do?"

"You have to ask? You really are dumb."

"Frank!"

"What? I'm serious! Even when you were acting a little weird about Jessica."

"Weird, huh?" I pushed away and crossed my arms. "You really want to go there?"

He eyed me and took a breath like he was going to make a smart remark. I could feel my determination rise. I knew he'd been a jerk, and that I'd been the nice one to drop it without a comment. *Just try it, buddy.*

The air in the room felt thick. Then his gaze dropped to the floor, and he sighed. "No. Really, I was a jerk."

I coughed in shock. "What?"

His gaze flicked up to meet mine. "When we were in high school, I think I never felt good enough. We'd hang out, and you'd tease me, and...." He sighed again and ran his hand through his hair. "Maybe I was testing you to see if you really liked me. If this was real." His hand panned between us. "And I'm sorry. I was being such a—"

"Seriously?" I interrupted.

"Yeah, I think, subconsciously, I was looking to see if you'd care. Wow. I sound so lame saying that out loud."

I settled back on the couch, my arms dropping to my sides. "You were trying to make me jealous."

"Uh." His eyes widened with fear. "Maybe?" He raised his hand. "I swear, I didn't do it on purpose, and I won't do it again. I guess, deep down, I just never thought I was in your ballpark."

"Frank, I honestly don't know how to feel about that." That wasn't exactly true. I did know how I felt—slightly offended—but I'd also never heard him discuss his insecurities like this before.

"I'm sorry. That's all I can say. I wish I hadn't acted that way." He snorted. "Jessica thought I was being weird, too."

"Did she? Where is she, now?"

"She's back home." His eyebrows puckered in a hang dog look. "Will you forgive me?"

It took me two seconds to decide. I offered him my hand and

yanked him up. "Yeah, of course. Now, come on. I'm practically starving here."

He sheepishly grinned and pulled me into a hug.

"Thank you for being so honest," I murmured into his chest.

He tipped my chin up to kiss me. "Thank you for being so safe to be honest with."

After a few more kisses, he dragged me into the kitchen. "Now, remember, I'm making dinner. You're doing dessert. You promised me that cheesecake, remember?"

I had promised it to him. I was determined to learn how to make it after the close call of nearly being banned from Sunny Acres. I could hardly wait until I perfected my recipe enough to present it to Cecelia.

Opening a cupboard, he started rummaging for a pan.

"To the right of you," I said.

"And the olive oil?"

I directed him to that and then the pepper when he asked.

He washed his hands, then rolled up his sleeves. It was kind of sexy. I perched on a chair next to him and watched.

"Whatcha cooking, good looking?" I teased.

He snorted and shook his head.

"What?" I asked, crossing my arms.

"Calling me good looking. I'm thinking you need your eyes checked." He pulled a package of steak from a bag. Within seconds, the steak was opened and sitting on a plate while he waited for the oil to heat.

"Nothing wrong with my eyes," I said. Then I doubted my own words as I watched him grab out the cinnamon. "Err, what are you doing?"

He glanced down at the spice in his hands and started to uncap it. "What?" he asked innocently.

"What are you doing?" My voice curled the last syllable into a near bird-like shriek. The spice bottle cast a warning shadow on the meat as he started to upturn it.

"What was it that you always said about me? Something about being a stick in the mud who needed to try new things?"

"I meant new things like paddle-boarding and snow-shoeing. Not ruining good meat."

His eye twinkled at me. "You're not the only one who can joke, shorty."

"This is a joke? You're not really using cinnamon?" I deadpanned.

His lip twerked slightly at the corner as he put the spice away, obviously pleased with himself.

"You need to leave joking to the professionals." I shook my head and gave him the stare-down.

His lip curved on the other side. I was impressed he actually smiled and grinned back.

"Well, you're smiling, so it was worth it," he said. "Now let me finish getting some cooking done here."

I leaned back in my chair, content. I was happy with how everything had worked out, and even happier that I was on my way to finally getting some real answers about Derek.

By the way, the dinner was awesome. The cheesecake needed some work, but I was starting to get a hang of this baking thing. If you'd like to try your hand at it, here's the recipe I used.

Cheesecake— First rule is to remember to prepare the ingredients ahead of time because you need to let the cold ingredients come to room temperature.

Crust—Toss a package and half of graham crackers (approximately 15 full-size crackers) into a zip-lock bag and crush them with a rolling pin until you have a little under two cups worth.

Mix those crumbs with 1/2 cup of melted butter, 1/4 tsp

cinnamon (this is where it's needed, not steak, Frank!) and 1/4 cup sugar. Press the crust mixture into the bottom and sides of a 10 inch springform pan.

Filling— Remember these all need to be room temperature. You need 1 cup of sugar, 2 1/2 tsps vanilla, 3 eggs, 3–8 ounce packages of regular, plain cream cheese, and one cup regular sour cream. (by regular I mean the full-fat versions)

Mix the cream cheese and sugar until well-blended. Add the vanilla and sour cream and blend together until smooth. Then, switching your mixer to low speed, add the eggs and continue to stir until lightly blended.

Pour into your crust and place in oven.

Bake for approximately one hour, ten minutes at 300 degrees. About 20 minutes into it, shield your crust with a pie crust shield or tin foil.

You can serve it with canned cherry pie filling, lemon curd, or strawberry sauce on the side. Yum!

Thanks for reading my latest adventure. Turn in to more Baker Street Mysteries. In the meantime, here are two more mystery series that can be read free with kindle unlimited.

Oceanside Hotel Cozy Mysteries

Booked For Murder

CEECEE JAMES

Deadly Reservation

Final Check Out

Fatal Vacancy

Suite Casualty

Angel Lake Cozy Mysteries

The Sweet Taste of Murder

The Bitter Taste of Betrayal

The Sour Taste of Suspicion

The Honeyed Taste of Deception

The Tempting Taste of Danger

The Frosty Taste of Scandal

Made in the USA
Monee, IL
04 August 2021

74922330R00132